"Keep your head down."

Everett pulled off the roadway onto a dirt path. "We're being followed."

It's him. The killer. She didn't give voice to her suspicion. Couldn't.

He stopped behind a thick stand of trees. "Stay here. I'll go check."

Seconds after he disappeared into the woods, brakes squealed in the distance. Cuddling the baby tighter, she heard a crack of a gunshot cut through the stillness.

A lump of fear filled her throat.

No. Surely Everett hadn't been shot. Then a new realization hit her. The shooter could follow the tire tracks. She and the baby were easy prey.

She stepped from the car and ran, clutching the baby close.

Leaves rustled behind her. Footfalls came closer. Her toe caught, she started to fall and someone grabbed her.

"I've got you."

It wasn't the killer, but Everett.

Debby Giusti is an award-winning Christian author who met and married her military husband at Fort Knox, Kentucky. Together they traveled the world, raised three wonderful children and have now settled in Atlanta, Georgia, where Debby spins tales of mystery and suspense that touch the heart and soul. Visit Debby online at debbygiusti.com; blog with her at seekerville.blogspot.com and craftieladiesofromance.blogspot.com; and email her at Debby@DebbyGiusti.com.

Books by Debby Giusti

Love Inspired Suspense

Military Investigations

The Officer's Secret
The Captain's Mission
The Colonel's Daughter
The General's Secretary
The Soldier's Sister
The Agent's Secret Past
Stranded
Person of Interest

Magnolia Medical

Countdown to Death
Protecting Her Child

Visit the Author Profile page at Harlequin.com for more titles.

PERSON OF INTEREST

DEBBY GIUSTI

 HARLEQUIN®LOVE INSPIRED® SUSPENSE

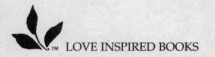 LOVE INSPIRED BOOKS

Recycling programs
for this product may
not exist in your area.

ISBN-13: 978-0-373-67697-2

Person of Interest

Copyright © 2015 by Deborah W. Giusti

www.Harlequin.com

Printed in U.S.A.

I love You, Lord, my strength,
Lord, my rock, my fortress, my deliverer,
My God, my rock of refuge,
my shield, my saving horn, my stronghold!
—*Psalms* 18:2

In thanksgiving for
The Seekers
My twelve Sisters in Christ
who spread God's message of
love and mercy
through their wonderful stories.

I give thanks to my God at every remembrance of you.
–Philippians 1:3

Tina Radcliffe

Mary Connealy

Janet Dean

Audra Harders

Ruth Logan Herne

Pam Hillman

Cara Lynn James

Myra Johnson

Glynna Kaye

Sandra Leesmith

Julie Lessman

Missy Tippens

ONE

Natalie Frazier's heart raced as she woke with a start and struggled to get her bearings. Blinking her way back to reality, she recognized the Joneses' living room on post at Fort Rickman, Georgia, instead of her own apartment in nearby Freemont.

Outside, wind tangled through the giant oaks. Branches creaked in the September night and scraped against the two-story brick quarters. The sound added to her unease as lightning flashed through the windows, followed by thunder that buffeted the house.

She closed the book that lay open on her lap and hesitated, listening for the baby's cry. Relieved that the little one hadn't awakened, she placed the textbook on the coffee table. *How to Manage the Middle School Classroom* was required reading for her teaching degree and had undoubtedly lulled her to sleep.

But what had awakened her?

Natalie had accepted the two-week nanny position caring for Lieutenant Wanda Jones's five-month-old daughter while Wanda was away for training, and she planned to use the time to catch up on her classwork.

As prior military, with six years on active duty under her belt, Natalie was usually unfazed by new circumstances. Tonight was different.

In hopes of calming her anxiety, she hurried into the foyer and insured the front door was locked before she stepped to the nearby window. Easing back the curtain, she stared for a long moment at the narrow, two-lane road that ran through the military housing area. A porch light from one of the duplexes across the street cast a yellow glow over the few cars parked at the curb.

Dropping the curtain, she flexed her shoulders to allay the tension in her neck and padded across the hardwood floor to the kitchen. The small, cozy room had seemed inviting this morning when she'd arrived. Wanda had coffee brewing and warm-from-the-oven cinnamon rolls to welcome her. The scent of the fresh brew and hot rolls had long since disappeared, leaving behind an emptiness that tugged at her heart. She and the baby were safe, yet something about the night was unsettling. Probably the darkness outside and the encroaching storm. Both caused her concern.

Opening the door to the attached one-car garage, she stared into the interior, seeing only her small sedan. Convinced her imagination was playing tricks on her, she shut the door and slipped the chain lock in place before she flipped off the kitchen light and retraced her steps into the main living-dining room combination.

She needed to check on Sofia. Natalie climbed the steep wooden stairway to the second floor and tiptoed into the nursery. The little one was asleep on her back, her cheeks plump and rosy.

Wanda had been concerned about leaving. With her husband—Sofia's father—deployed to the Middle East, the female lieutenant had weighed accepting a two-week school assignment at Fort Hood that was good for her military career but hard on a new mom forced to leave her infant daughter.

Natalie and Wanda had been stationed together in Germany and had reconnected after Natalie had moved to nearby Freemont. Natalie was happy to help, and the arrangement would be good for both of them. Wanda needed child care, and Natalie wanted time to study away from her cramped apartment and moody roommate.

Denise Lang had become increasingly irritable over the past two months. Natalie blamed her roommate's new boyfriend, who insisted Denise keep their relationship under wraps. The secrecy was taking a toll on her and impacted her relationship with Natalie.

Pulling the receiving blanket up around Sofia's shoulders, Natalie smiled at the precious child and returned to the hallway on her way to the guest room. The sound of raised voices from the adjoining quarters next door stopped her at the top of the stairs.

She should have asked Wanda about the neighbors. All she'd provided had been the woman's first name and her phone number. Natalie didn't even know the couple's last name. Surely the bickering wasn't a regular occurrence.

Thunder rolled overhead, and rain drummed against the roof. The voices grew louder as the storm intensified. Although the shared wall between the two sets of quarters prevented Natalie from understanding what was said, the harsh tones signaled escalating conflict.

A woman screamed.

Something crashed against the wall.

Natalie gasped and took a step back. Her pulse raced.

Another crash and a second scream were followed by a series of thumps as if something—or someone—had fallen down the stairway.

Heart in her throat, Natalie checked again to be certain Sofia was asleep before she ran downstairs and opened the front door. The storm had unleashed its fury with strong winds and torrential rain. Her voice of reason told her to stay dry and mind her own business, but her need to help overrode the warning.

Ignoring the deluge, she raced next door and climbed the steps to the neighbor's porch. In her haste, she slipped, then steadied herself and pounded on the door.

"Is someone hurt?"

Feeling exposed, she glanced over her shoulder, expecting to see the neighbors spilling from the quarters across the street. As loud as the woman's scream had been, they should have heard her, as well. Another clap of thunder made her realize the woman's cries had been masked by the storm.

Again, Natalie knocked and raised her voice. "Do you need help?"

The door remained closed.

Envisioning a tragic scene inside, she hurried back to the Joneses' quarters, wiped the rain from her face and reached for the phone. Her hands shook as she searched through the list of emergency numbers Wanda had left. Finding the military police, she tapped in the digits and waited impatiently for someone to answer, then explained the situation.

"I'll send a squad car," the MP said.

"Hurry."

Everett Kohl shoved his travel toiletry kit into his duffel and zipped it shut with a smile. Tomorrow he'd be heading to North Georgia for two weeks of R&R and a chance to help Uncle Harry get his mountain cabin ready to put on the market to sell. Everett had half a notion to buy the place himself. But, first, he wanted to assess the structure and tend to the repairs that needed to be done.

Much as he loved his uncle, Harry's age and stubbornness could be a problem, especially since he was trading the North Georgia mountains for an assisted-living complex in the metro Atlanta area. The timing was right, but his uncle saw it as losing his independence and a way of life he had enjoyed for over eighty years. Everett hoped to soothe the transition and ease his uncle's concerns about the change.

Grateful the rain had stopped and the storm subsided, Everett whistled as he hurried to his SUV and threw his duffel in the rear. Nothing would delay him in the morning. He'd packed, filled his gas tank and was ready to lock up his bachelor officer's quarters and drive north.

Retracing his steps, he checked his watch. Almost midnight. He'd catch some shut-eye and rise before dawn to skirt the morning traffic in Atlanta, two hours north, on his way to the mountains.

He entered his BOQ apartment just as his cell rang. Glancing at the screen, he saw Special Agent Frank Gallagher's name displayed. The chief was out of town and Frank was in charge.

"I've already signed out on leave," Everett said in lieu of a greeting.

"We've got an incident that needs your finesse."

"You say the nicest things, but buttering me up won't work. The next trip I take will be out the front gate in the morning. I'll wave as I pass CID Headquarters on my way off post."

"The military police just called with a

heads-up. Someone reported hearing a domestic squabble at Mason Yates's quarters."

Everett groaned inwardly and shoved the cell closer to his ear. Domestic violence was never pretty and especially troublesome when a fellow agent was involved. "I'm listening."

"A woman named Natalie Frazier heard arguing coming from the other side of her duplex and called in the report. I told the MP we'd check it out, but I can't believe Mason would hurt his wife. If it's bogus, we go home relieved that his name doesn't end up on the commanding general's desk tomorrow morning."

"We owe the MPs for contacting us."

"Exactly. Call me optimistic, but I'm hoping the neighbor's imagination was working overtime due to the storm. If it's a mistaken call, you'll be home sawing logs before you can say 'take care of our own' three times."

"Give me the address, I'll meet you there."

Frank provided the street and quarters number.

"Didn't Mason move into military housing a few weeks ago?" Everett remembered the newcomer talking about signing for quarters.

"Three weeks to be exact. As I recall, his

wife stayed with his sister in Decatur, Georgia, until quarters were available."

Everett had arrived at Fort Rickman six months earlier, so he wasn't an old-timer on post. He and Frank had been stationed together years earlier, along with Special Agent Colby Voss, which had made his transition to Fort Rickman an easy one.

Mason reported to post eight weeks ago. Since then, he had seemed withdrawn and less than willing to join in the office camaraderie that often relieved the stress of working long hours on felony cases for the military. Probably a loner by nature or maybe a bit aloof. That he outranked the other special agents might have bearing on his attitude, especially if he hoped to step into the chief's shoes. Chief Agent-in-Charge Craig Wilson had led the CID office at Fort Rickman for nearly three years. Even if Uncle Sam considered him ready for a new assignment, no one wanted the chief to be reassigned.

Mason was an unknown, which gave Everett pause.

"I'm trusting this ends well," he said in closing.

"Agreed," Frank added. "I'll meet you there."

The housing area wasn't far, and Everett was

the first to arrive. He pulled to the curb and spotted headlights in his rearview mirror, then stepped out and waited for Frank.

"The report came from that side of the duplex," Frank pointed to Quarters A. "Let's talk to Mason before we question the neighbor." Frank was the lead on this call, with Everett along as another set of eyes if need be.

Both agents climbed the front steps. Frank knocked on the door. "Special Agent Frank Gallagher, CID." He glanced at Everett before adding. "Mason, it's Frank. Everett's with me. Everything okay?"

He tapped the door again.

Everett glanced at the duplex across the street. A light went on in an upstairs window.

"I'll check the rear." Starting down the steps, he heard a door creak open and turned to find the neighbor in Quarters A standing backlit in her doorway.

Long, shoulder-length black hair, slender build. Probably 110 to 115 pounds and five-four or five-five.

She stepped onto the porch. Oval face, big eyes drawn with concern, her mouth angled downward in a frown.

"We're with the CID, ma'am. I'm Special

Agent Kohl," he said as introduction. "You called in the report?"

She glanced at her watch. "About fifteen minutes ago. I haven't heard anything since then."

"What did you hear earlier?"

"Raised voices and two screams, followed by thumping, as if someone had fallen down the stairs."

Everett nodded. "Wait inside, ma'am. I'll need more information after we make contact with the residents."

Walking through the wet grass, he rounded the house, flicking his gaze over the large side yard and the rear access road. Headlights signaled an approaching vehicle. A dark blue sedan screeched to a stop.

Mason lunged from the car, wearing running shorts and a gray Army T-shirt damp with sweat. Eyes wide, he glanced at Everett, then turned his focus to his quarters.

"It's Tammy, isn't it? What happened? Is she hurt?" Breathless, he raced to the back door.

"A neighbor heard screams." Everett hated being the bearer of bad news.

"She called me, distraught. I heard a voice in the background." Mason pushed open the door and charged into the kitchen.

Everett followed. Unwashed dishes sat in the sink.

"Tammy, where are you?" Mason ran through the living room, then rounded the corner into the foyer. Stopping short, he staggered to brace himself against the wall.

"No!"

Everett's gut tightened. A woman lay sprawled at the foot of the stairs, her face contorted in death. Blood pooled under her head.

He felt her neck, knowing instinctively he wouldn't find a pulse.

Mason fell to the floor and reached for his wife, a scream keening from deep within him.

"Don't touch—" Everett couldn't warn Mason fast enough.

The husband's broken sobs echoed in the quarters.

Everett had been at too many crime scenes, but none as wrenching as Mason holding his wife's lifeless body.

He pulled a handkerchief from his pocket and opened the front door. Frank stepped inside, face tight and eyes brimming with the same emotion Everett felt as they shook their heads with regret. Both special agents were aware of the significance of Mason's arrival on-site. If he hadn't been home, then someone else had argued with his wife. Someone who may have pushed or shoved or thrown Tammy Yates down the stairs to her death.

Everett raised his cell and called CID Headquarters. "Notify the military police. We'll need a crime-scene investigation team, ambulance and the medical examiner."

Frank patted Mason's shoulder. "Come on, buddy. Let's get you into the other room. The MPs are on the way along with the ME."

Mason shook off the attempt to comfort him. "Tammy," he moaned, pulling his wife even closer into his arms.

"You need to step away from your wife. Remember, we have to preserve evidence if we're going to catch this guy. Come on, buddy. Let's head into the other room."

Mason shrugged out of Frank's hold and glanced at the open doorway. His face twisted in rage.

"What's she doing here?"

Everett turned to see the neighbor cover her mouth and muffle a cry of disbelief. Fear flared from her eyes.

"Ma'am, I asked you to remain in your quarters."

She pointed a finger at Mason, the distraught husband holding his wife's bloodied body, and screamed.

TWO

Natalie ran back to the Joneses' quarters, unable to take in more of the death scene. The horrendous sight stuck in her mind, and she couldn't erase the image of the woman lying at the bottom on the stairs.

Seeing who clutched the woman's bloodied body was even more unsettling. She hadn't expected Mason Yates to be the neighbor next door. Her stomach rolled, recalling his steely eyes and accusing glare that brought back memories she wanted to forget.

Locking the door behind her, Natalie raced to the downstairs half bath and ran water in the sink. Pumping a large dollop of liquid soap into her palm, she lathered her hands and tried to wash off the blood she kept seeing.

Although she hadn't entered the Yateses' quarters, she felt soiled and defiled. Scrubbing with soap and rinsing her hands in the hot tap water did little to change the feeling.

Her reflection stared back at her from the mirror. Black hair, still damp with rain, tumbled around her shoulders in disarray, and her eyes, puffy from her earlier sleep, appeared as anxious as she felt.

Worried about the baby, she dried her hands and raced upstairs, trying to keep her footfalls light. She felt vulnerable, knowing the men on the opposite side of the wall would hear her as she climbed the stairs.

Relieved to find Sofia still asleep, Natalie rubbed the back of her hand over the baby's soft cheek, needing contact with goodness and purity after what she'd seen.

She shook her head and tried to calm her racing heart, but all she could think of was the woman who had died. Her mouth gaped open as if the scream Natalie had heard had carried down the stairs with her. Death was supposed to be peaceful, but the neighbor's death had been anything but.

Blood was smeared along the wall and down the stairs, pooling under her head. The sights had brought back too many memories of another woman who had died in Germany. The similarity was frightening.

Hurrying downstairs, Natalie stopped in the foyer and shivered, realizing she was standing in the exact spot where the victim's body lay in Quarters B. Sirens sounded in the distance, and flashing lights filtered through the gauze curtains.

She glanced out the window. Two military police squad cars pulled to the curb. An ambulance followed. The medical personnel were too late to save the woman and would, instead, transport her body to the morgue.

A knock sounded at the door.

Swallowing the lump that filled her throat, Natalie peered through the peephole. The CID special agent she'd spoken with earlier stood on the porch.

Needing to control her emotions, she ran her fingers through her hair and sighed, thinking of the tangled web into which she'd stepped.

If only she could turn to God, but He'd never taken an interest in her. Not in Detroit growing up, not with a mother whose care bordered on abuse, not with a father who liked the bottle more than he liked his only child. God hadn't helped her then. He wouldn't help her now.

Her breath hitched when she opened the door. Earlier, she hadn't realized how broad the special agent's shoulders were or the deep brown of his eyes. Even through the screen door, they appeared rimmed with concern. She couldn't let down her guard, no matter how sympathetic the agent seemed.

She had to be strong and take care of herself. She'd done it before. She could do it again.

At least, she hoped she could.

Plus, she couldn't let anything or anyone harm Sofia. The baby's needs came before her own, and Sofia's safety was Natalie's main concern for the next two weeks.

Despite the tragic crime scene Everett had just left, he couldn't help but be taken in by the woman who answered his knock at Quarters 324-A. She was pretty, with dark brows and pensive eyes, a slender nose and full cheeks now pale and drawn, like her mouth. Even her shoulders seemed weighted down, no doubt from what she'd seen. Death was never pretty, and Mrs. Yates's life had come to a traumatic end.

While the ME tended to the body and the crime-scene team looked for evidence, Everett needed to question the neighbor.

Frank was continuing to quiz Mason. He had been running in the training area when his wife had fallen to her death.

In shock and visibly grieving, Mason had been forthcoming about the evening he and Mrs. Yates had spent together. She had prepared a light meal, they had watched a favorite TV show, and soon thereafter, he had left, as he often did, for a nighttime jog. From the many photos displayed in the home, they appeared to have been a loving couple, but things weren't always as they seemed.

Case in point, the attractive woman staring at Everett through the screen door. She appeared totally confused and upset. Had she seen or heard more than raised voices and thumps against the wall?

Although he had introduced himself earlier, he doubted the woman had focused on his name when she was worried about her neighbor. Again, he held up his badge. Following protocol was always good, especially tonight when a woman had died so tragically.

"Everett Kohl, Criminal Investigation Division. I'd like to ask you some questions."

She pushed open the screen door. "Come in."

The house was tidy and nicely furnished with a leather couch and two chairs covered in a flowered pattern.

A number of side tables held pretty knick-knacks and photos of a baby. "Your child?"

She shook her head. "Sofia's the daughter of Lieutenant Terrance Jones and his wife, Wanda. She's also a lieutenant."

"You're visiting the Joneses?"

"I'm the nanny, at least for the next two weeks. Wanda's TDY at Fort Hood."

"What about her husband?"

"He's deployed to Afghanistan." She pointed him toward the living area. "Shall we sit down? I have a feeling this might take time."

"Hopefully not too long." He lowered himself onto the couch. The leather was cool to his touch. He drew a tablet and pen from the pocket of his jacket. "If you don't mind, I'll take a few notes."

"Of course."

"Let's start with your name."

"Natalie Frazier. I'm prior military, served for six years and now live in Freemont."

"Marital status?"

"I'm single."

She seemed willing to provide information. A good sign. "You said you were caring for the Joneses' daughter."

"That's right."

"You work as a nanny?"

"I started this morning as a favor to Wanda. She's taking an army training class at Fort Hood that begins in a few days and didn't have anyone to care for her child. I'm finishing the last course for my teaching degree and hope to find a job in the local schools. The nanny position came at the right time."

He noticed the textbook on the coffee table. "How did you meet Lieutenant Jones?"

"We knew each other in Germany. That was my last duty station. Wanda and I were both taking night classes for our degrees. I transferred back to Fort Rickman, liked the area and decided not to reenlist."

"And home is?"

She stared at him as if she didn't understand. "Freemont is currently my home. I live at 2010 Pinegate Circle. You probably want my phone number."

He nodded, made note of the cell number she provided and then rephrased his earlier question.

"Where was home before the military?

"Where did I grow up?" She hesitated. "I was raised in Detroit."

The inner city had crumbled over the past decade into a no-man's land. The suburbs still held on to hope of regeneration, but the downtown looked worse than some of the bombed-out areas in Afghanistan.

As if reading his mind, her voice took on a defensive edge. "I joined the army to make a life for myself, Special Agent Kohl, and I hardly see how where I grew up has bearing on what happened tonight."

"Yes, ma'am." He looked down at his notebook. "Let's go back to this evening. Could you tell me what you heard?"

"Pounding against the wall. A woman screamed twice, followed by a thumping sound." She crossed her arms and hugged herself as if to find comfort. "It sounded like someone was falling down the stairs."

"There was a storm," he prompted. "Lightning, thunder, heavy rain. Could you have mistaken the rumble of thunder for sounds you thought came from the adjoining quarters?"

She bristled. "I know what thunder sounds like."

"Of course you do."

Her shoulders sagged and her assuredness ebbed. "I was studying for an exam and had evidently fallen asleep."

"Here in the living room?"

"That's right. Something woke me. Maybe the storm. Maybe something else. Like raised voices or a crash against the wall."

Natalie continued to chronicle what had provoked her call. "I heard voices that escalated into a heated argument, although I couldn't make out what was being said."

"Could you determine if the voices were male or female?"

"Not really, although one of them sounded far more aggressive and seemingly male."

"Seemingly?"

"It was deeper, raised and more insistent. The argument kept escalating. When something crashed against the wall, I immediately thought of domestic abuse."

"How many times did something crash against the wall?"

"Two times, maybe three."

He pursed his lips. "You're not sure?"

"Two hits. Both followed by a scream. I knew something bad was happening."

"Did you pound on the wall or call out to see if anyone needed help?"

"Not at that point." She raised her brow as if worried she hadn't reacted appropriately. "Do you think I should have?"

"Ma'am, I can't tell you what you should have done."

She sighed. "I doubt they would have heard me."

"Then what happened?"

"A series of thumps sounded down the stairs. I knew someone had fallen or had been pushed."

"Is that when you called the police?"

"First I went outside and banged on their door."

"Did anyone respond to your knock?"

"Regrettably, no." She let out a breath. "Common sense took over when I realized how vulnerable I was, especially since I had Sofia and her safety to think about. And I needed to get back here as soon as possible."

"Did you feel threatened at any time?"

"Not personally, just upset that something tragic had happened."

"What did you think had happened, ma'am?"

"That the woman had been pushed down the stairs, which seems to be what *did* happen."

"That's one possibility."

"Surely you don't think she slipped and fell?"

"Nothing has been ruled out at this point."

Natalie sat up straighter and squared her slender shoulders. "You work with him, don't you?"

"Him?"

"Mason Yates. The husband. Isn't the husband usually the most likely suspect?"

Everett tensed. "There will be an investigation before anyone is charged, if this even was a crime. We're not sure Special Agent Yates was in the house at the time Mrs. Yates fell."

"I heard him."

"You heard a voice—" he glanced at his notes "—a *seemingly* male voice—through an insulated wall."

"You don't believe me?"

"I don't disbelieve you. I'm just getting information. What happened after you knocked on the Yateses' door?"

"I ran back here and called the military police, and then I waited for someone to arrive, which you did."

"Did you hear any other noise from the house?"

"No.

"Did you look out the window?"

"I glanced at the street. I had checked the doors to insure they were locked earlier and then relocked the front door when I came back inside."

"Did you hear a door close anywhere in the area? What about a car engine or a car door slamming?"

"I heard nothing. The storm had passed, and even the rain had stopped by the time you arrived."

"Did Wanda Jones provide information about her neighbors?"

"Only Mrs. Yates's first name and phone number. But I recognized Special Agent Yates."

"How so?"

"I worked for him in Germany for the last six months of my assignment there."

Everett bit down on his jaw to hold himself in check. He hadn't expected the connection. Willing his voice to remain calm, he asked, "At CID Headquarters in Vilseck?"

She nodded. "They were short staffed. I worked as a personnel clerk and was brought in to handle paperwork."

"What was your relationship with Mason Yates in Germany?"

"We didn't have a relationship. He was a CID agent. I was an E-5 personnel clerk."

"Did you meet socially?"

"Of course not."

"Did you work long hours or work together on the weekends?"

She cocked her brow. "I'm not sure where this is headed."

"I'm just interested in how well you knew Agent Yates."

"I knew him only as a CID agent, not socially. We hardly talked unless he needed paperwork dealing with personnel."

"Did you know Mrs. Yates?"

"She came to the office once, as I recall. I was introduced to her."

"Agent Yates introduced you?"

"I believe so, although I can't say for sure."

"You don't remember?"

"I met a lot of people in Germany. I don't remember every situation."

"Did you realize the Yateses lived next door to the Joneses when you accepted the babysitting position?"

She shook her head. "I didn't even know they had transferred to Fort Rickman."

"No one notified you from Germany when Special Agent Yates was reassigned?"

"Perhaps you didn't hear me." She lifted her chin. "I wasn't aware the Yateses had left Europe."

"I understand." He checked his notes.

"You mentioned that you couldn't determine specifically if the voices were male or female. Is that correct?"

"It is." She hesitated and raised her brow. "Although one of the voices sounded male. It could have been Mason Yates."

"Could have been or was?"

"I…I'm not sure."

Everett closed his notebook. He didn't know what to think about the nanny. She had called in a domestic violence dispute when she talked to the military police, yet according to Mason's own account, he had been running on a track in the training area. Somewhat unusual to do PT at night, but physical training was important to the military. If Mason liked to run at night, so be it. The track was lit, and a number of soldiers took advantage of the cool evenings to exercise. Video cameras were posted in the area, which would confirm his alibi.

Everett had checked Mason's cell phone log and found a call from his wife, just as the distraught husband had claimed when he'd leaped from his car and raced toward his house. The wife's cell log also confirmed that a call had been made, a call that Mason said had spurred him to hurry home.

The husband seemed to be telling the truth,

not that Natalie Frazier wasn't. More than likely, she had heard bickering. If Mason wasn't at home, then the more aggressive voice she presumed was male had to have belonged to someone else. Someone who had argued with Mrs. Yates and perhaps caused her death.

"Thank you, Ms. Frazier." Everett stood to leave. "I'll be in touch."

"You know where to find me."

"Yes, ma'am." He dug in his pocket and handed her his business card. "Be sure to call me if you think of anything else."

He needed to check on the nanny's tour of duty in Germany and find out how well she knew both Mason and his wife. Her sudden arrival on post the day of Mrs. Yates's death seemed questionable, especially since she'd worked with Mason.

The air was heavy with humidity as he walked outside. Overhead, a sliver of moon peered through the clouds. Cicadas and tree frogs croaked in the night.

A man hurried across the street. Tall, slender, early thirties. "Mind telling me what's going on?" he asked, his face drawn with concern.

Everett flashed his CID identification. "Could I have your name, sir?"

"Lieutenant Bobby Slade." He pointed over his shoulder to the duplex where Everett had seen the light come on earlier. "I live in 325-B. Something bad must have happened."

"Did you notice anything unusual this evening?"

The guy raked his hand over his short hair and let out a stiff breath. "Unusual." He thought for a long moment. "No, not really. I noticed a different car parked in the alleyway behind the Yateses' quarters earlier. Probably a friend."

"Can you remember the make and model of car?"

He shook his head. "'Fraid not. I didn't know it would be important. Did someone get hurt?"

"Mrs. Yates fell."

"Oh, man, I'm sorry. If there's anything my wife or I can do…"

"Why don't you go back inside, sir. Someone from the military police will want to talk to you later about that car."

"You mean, the fall wasn't accidental?"

"We'll contact you, sir."

The guy nodded and hurried back to his quarters. An inquisitive neighbor who saw a car in the area. Not much, but Everett made note of the information on his tablet. Sometimes the smallest detail could have bearing on a case.

He raised his cell and called Frank, who answered on the second ring.

"Yeah, Rett. What's up?"

"We've got an inquisitive neighbor across the street. Lieutenant Bobby Slade. Quarters 325-B. The guy saw a car parked behind the Yateses' home today. You might want the MPs to question him when they do their door-to-door."

"Is that the reason you called?"

"Negative. I talked to the nanny. Interesting development that I don't want Mason to overhear."

"Where are you?"

"On the sidewalk outside."

Frank chuckled. "Not to worry. Mason's in the latrine, and I'm in the kitchen out of earshot. What'd you find out?"

"Natalie Frazier is prior service. You'll never guess her last duty station."

"Vilseck, Germany," Frank said. "She worked as a personnel specialist in the CID office."

"Mason told you?"

"That's right. He said she was a loner, kind of aloof."

Which is exactly how Everett would describe Mason.

"He's grieving, having a hard time putting his thoughts together," Frank continued. "Seeing Ms. Frazier was a complete surprise. Mason didn't know she was in the area."

Everett glanced at the sky. Dark clouds rolled past the moon, blocking its light. "Strange coincidence that she'd show up on post the night Tammy Yates dies."

"You think she's involved?"

He sighed. At this point, he didn't know what to think. "Just wondering how this investigation will play out."

"Do you still plan to go on leave in the morning?"

"I'll stick around and give you a hand."

"Appreciate the help."

"You stood by me," Everett said, remembering Frank being there when he'd needed a friend. "I'll always be grateful."

"Don't blame yourself."

"I should have kept the investigation open, Frank."

"You were following orders."

"That doesn't help me sleep at night."

Everett disconnected and glanced again at Quarters 324-A. Maybe he was being overly cautious, but he would keep his eye on the attractive nanny. Natalie could be an innocent bystander, or she could play an important role in a murder investigation.

...quarters, but knew she watched for her safety...
...him risk charges, pulling out his medicine...
...trying to... The curtailing drapes closed. Not that...
...it would matter much now.

THREE

Natalie peered through the window and watched first the ambulance and then one of the two patrol cars pull away from the curb and head out of the housing area. Her head throbbed with tension that had escalated since she'd first awakened on the couch. What would she do if Mason remained behind after the crime-scene team left?

As if in response to her concern, he stepped from his quarters and approached the SUV parked in front of the house. Special Agent Everett Kohl walked next to him and opened the passenger door and shut it with a slam once Mason had climbed inside.

Rounding the front of the vehicle, Special Agent Kohl glanced at the duplex. He hesitated for a long moment, and then as she watched, he walked briskly up the sidewalk and climbed the stairs to the Joneses' front porch. She opened the door before he knocked.

"Do you have more questions?" Natalie asked.

"I wanted to let you know Special Agent Yates will be staying at the Lodge on post for the next few days. The military police will question the other neighbors either later tonight or in the morning. We'll follow up on each bit of evidence and information until we get to the truth."

She appreciated his thoughtfulness. "Thank you for letting me know."

"You have my card. Don't hesitate to contact me if you remember anything else." He paused for a long moment and stared at her through pensive eyes. "You shouldn't have any problems, but if you feel threatened, just call."

Natalie reached for his business card that she'd placed on the side table by the door and glanced again at his name and the accompanying phone numbers, unwilling to let him see the confusion she felt. She'd been on her own for so long, taking care of herself, that she didn't know how to respond. His concern for her well-being touched her, but she couldn't let down her guard, even if Special Agent Kohl seemed sincere.

Shoving his card into the pocket of her jeans, she willed her expression to remain neutral. "I'll call if there's a problem."

He nodded, seemingly satisfied with her response, and returned to his SUV.

Climbing behind the wheel, he started the engine and then stared again at the doorway where she still stood. Mason glanced up from the passenger seat. She couldn't make out his expression, but she sensed hostility in his gaze. Unwilling to let either man destroy her fragile composure, she closed the door before the car drove away.

A military post was a tight-knit community. News of Mrs. Yates's death would quickly spread. Natalie didn't want Wanda Jones to hear about the tragedy from someone else.

Reaching for her cell, Natalie found the number in her contact information and hit Call. Wanda sounded groggy with sleep when she answered.

"Sofia's fine," Natalie immediately assured her, "but I wanted you to know about your neighbor." She recounted what had happened and tried to calm Wanda, who became upset once she heard the news.

"I'm flying home tomorrow." The mother's voice bordered on hysteria.

"What about your class?"

"Nothing's as important as my child. I'll explain the situation. The instructors will have to understand that I need to be with my baby."

"Call me after you have your flight information."

"I don't feel good about you staying there tonight, Natalie. If someone killed Tammy, what's to stop them from striking again?"

"I've locked the doors. One of the special agents investigating the case gave me his number in case I need help."

"That's all well and good, but I want Sofia out of harm's way. We've got a small fishing cabin a few miles north of Freemont. There's a crib and some baby supplies so you and Sofia should be fine there. Plus, Terrance keeps a rifle in the coat closet. A box of ammo is on the top shelf."

"Wanda, you're scaring me."

"You need to take precautions. I'll fly home tomorrow and meet you there. The key to the cabin is in the top drawer of the buffet in the dining area. You'll also find a map with directions."

"Are you sure?"

"I'm positive. You and Sofia will be safe at

the cabin. I'll call you when I have my flight information."

Wanda's insistence that she take the baby off post darkened Natalie's mood even more. Fleeing Fort Rickman didn't sound like a wise decision, especially this late at night.

To clear her mind, Natalie climbed the stairs to the baby's room, finding comfort in the sweet innocence of the small infant. Standing at the side of the crib, she gazed down at the baby's face and tiny hands. Knowing Sofia was completely oblivious to the turmoil that surrounded them tonight brought a sense of calm to Natalie's unrest.

The house phone rang, causing the baby to stir. Natalie hurried into the master bedroom and reached for the receiver.

"The Joneses' residence."

Silence.

She pushed the phone closer to her ear. "Hello?"

No response.

Natalie disconnected. She didn't need prank calls, especially tonight.

Again the phone rang. She snatched it from the cradle and raised it to her ear.

"Natalie?" A garbled voice, as if the caller were masking his voice.

Could it be Mason? Repulsion filled her. And fear.

Her heart raced and her hands trembled as she disconnected.

Straightening her shoulders, she strained to draw air into her lungs. Wanda was right. She and Sofia needed to leave post and hide out until the killer was apprehended.

Natalie hurried into the guest bedroom, grateful she hadn't unpacked earlier today. Grabbing her suitcase and small tote, she dropped both in the hallway and returned to the baby's room. Wanda had filled a large diaper bag for when Natalie took the child on an outing. Unsure how many supplies she'd find at the cabin, she stuffed even more diapers into the bag and filled a second tote with onesies, sleepers and prepared bottles of formula. Receiving blankets were the final items she included before making two trips downstairs with the luggage and totes.

Peering out the front window, she noticed the last of the emergency responders preparing to leave. As much as she wanted to contact Everett Kohl, the CID was a tight organization. Natalie didn't stand a chance of changing anyone's mind about Mason. If only they'd look closer into his wife's death instead of giving their colleague a free pass.

After placing the bags in her car, she checked the car seat Wanda had helped her install, then hurriedly returned to the house. With a determine sigh, she climbed the stairs and lifted the sleeping baby into her arms. She'd never had her own child, but her maternal instincts kicked into high gear. No one would hurt this baby.

Returning to her car, she settled Sofia into the carrier and attached the harness before she opened the garage door and backed onto the driveway. Glancing at the neighboring homes, she wondered how soon people would be aware of what had happened tonight. Once the MPs made their rounds, the news would spread up and down the street, causing unrest and concern.

Poor Tammy Yates. She didn't deserve to die. Neither had the woman in Germany.

Natalie hated running scared. She'd run before, from her father's abusive drunkenness and from a scandal that meant the end of her time in the military. A scandal that had involved Mason. And now, she was running from a murderer.

She thought of Everett Kohl's strong shoulders and the concern she'd seen in his gaze, and for half a heartbeat, she wished she could turn to him, but common sense won out.

She couldn't trust Everett Kohl.

She couldn't trust anyone.

Everett watched the garage open at the Joneses' quarters. A red sedan backed onto the driveway. Natalie hurried from the car and lowered the garage door before she drove out of the housing area.

After dropping Mason at the Lodge on post, Everett had circled back to the duplex and parked farther down the street to keep an eye on the two homes. Not that he had expected Natalie Frazier to flee. He had been more concerned for her safety. If someone had broken into the B side of the duplex and killed one woman, the killer could easily return to kill again.

Everett had to insure he didn't leave a stone unturned. He'd learned his lesson the hard way. The guilt still hung heavy on his shoulders.

He followed the small compact car at a distance as it left post through the Fort Rickman main gate and headed into nearby Freemont. On the far side of town, it stopped at an apartment complex.

Holding the baby in her arms, Natalie unlocked the bottom apartment door and disappeared for a few seconds before returning to the car. Everett made note of the address as she drove away.

Surprised when his cell rang, he saw Frank's name on the screen. "I was ready to call you," he said in greeting. "I'm following Natalie Frazier. She's got the baby and is driving north through Freemont. It appears she's headed to the interstate. I want to apprehend her before she hits the highway."

"Negative," Frank insisted. "Tail her but don't apprehend. I just called Lieutenant Jones to notify her of her neighbor's death. The lieutenant had spoken with the nanny earlier and had encouraged her to take the baby someplace safe."

"Did the mother mention a destination?"

"She talked about a fishing cabin north of Freemont but refused to provide more information. Stay on Ms. Frazier's tail. I want to know the exact location of the cabin and where that baby is at all times. Lieutenant Jones plans to return to Fort Rickman tomorrow. Once baby and mom are reunited, I'll breathe a sigh of relief."

"What about the nanny?"

"Lieutenant Jones is convinced she'll take good care of her daughter. That's my hope, as well, but it seems more than a coincidence, as you mentioned, to have her show up on post the day Tammy Yates dies."

"Natalie made a quick stop at her apartment in Freemont. Might be worth checking." Everett provided the address.

"Will do. Don't let her out of your sight. If Mrs. Yates's death is a homicide, we have a killer on the loose. We don't need anyone else hurt."

Everett disconnected. So much for his two-week vacation. Right now, he had to keep tabs on the red sedan and find out where Natalie planned to hole up, so he could keep nanny and baby safe.

Natalie saw the tail just as she turned into the narrow dirt road that led to the fishing cabin. She cut the lights and pulled to a stop at the side of the small wooden structure.

Knowing Sofia would be safer in her car seat, Natalie let the baby sleep while she dashed inside. Everything was as Wanda had mentioned, including the hunting rifle in the closet. Natalie found the ammo and loaded the weapon, then retraced her steps and hid in the underbrush until the car turned onto the dirt path.

Her heart pounded. She hadn't expected Mason to follow her. As the SUV drew closer, she crawled from the foliage, holding the rifle in her arms. The vehicle skidded to a stop.

"Get out, Mason," she screamed, aiming the gun at the shadowed outline of the man behind the wheel.

The door opened and long legs stepped to the ground, followed by a muscular chest, square jaw and dark eyes that stared at her with a perturbed frown.

"Lower that weapon before you hurt someone," he warned.

Not Mason.

Everett Kohl.

Did she need to fear him, as well?

Everett didn't like being one-upped, especially by a woman who looked light as a feather and about as threatening. Except for the Winchester .30-30.

A good rifle for hunting deer, and not the type of weapon a criminal would carry. Although it could do serious damage if she decided to pull the trigger.

Even with the rifle, Everett was confident

he could overpower her, but he wanted her to trust him. Allowing the nanny to think she was in control would be the best strategy to earn that trust, at least for now. Plus, he was packing a SIG Sauer under his jacket and a J-Frame Smith & Wesson strapped to his ankle. Hopefully, she didn't realize special agents were always armed.

A baby's cry cut through the darkness.

Seeing the concern on Natalie's face, he stepped toward the car and peered at the baby in the rear. "Someone's not happy."

"She's probably wet and hungry." Natalie motioned to the cabin. "Head for the porch and don't do anything stupid."

He pointed to the rifle. "You wouldn't use that, would you?"

She cocked her hip and tried to look defiant. "Don't tempt me."

"Shooting a law enforcement officer carries a stiff penalty that would end your hopes for a career in education, Ms. Frazier."

"It's Natalie, and I know what I'm doing."

"If so, then—"

"Then why am I holding you at gunpoint?"

He nodded. "Exactly."

"Because you followed me here, and I need to know why."

"To insure your safety."

"Wrong answer."

"But truthful." He titled his head. "Tell me why you're frightened of Mason?"

"You won't believe me."

"If you have information about Mrs. Yates's murder, why didn't you tell me earlier?"

"I made a mistake." Natalie's bravado deflated. "I had two prank phone calls on the Joneses' landline. I think they were from Mason."

"What?"

"When I saw headlights, I thought he had followed me here."

Pulling in a deep breath, Everett nodded. "You've got my attention. I'll meet you on the porch. But watch that rifle. I wouldn't want it to go off accidentally."

"Don't worry, Mr. Kohl. I've got everything under control."

Everett would have laughed if the situation weren't so dicey. "It's Everett."

Again, Sofia let out a bellow.

As he walked toward the cabin, he glanced over his shoulder. The nanny had placed the rifle on the ground to free her hands. She plucked Sofia from the backseat of her car and struggled to balance the baby and the diaper bag.

Natalie frowned when she looked up and found him staring at her.

He retraced his steps and held out his hands. "You're exhausted and loaded down. How 'bout I take the diaper bag and baby. You keep the gun."

Her brow lifted, but she didn't object as he reached for Sofia and nestled the baby against his shoulder. With his free hand, he grabbed the diaper bag.

"I'll meet you inside." He hurriedly climbed the steps and entered the rustic cabin. A stacked-stone fireplace sat to the right. The kitchen and eating area were on the left. A couch and two easy chairs filled the center of the room. An open door revealed a bedroom in the rear, and a second, smaller room with a crib and changer, which was where he headed.

Everett felt a swell of gratitude for his sister, who had let him help when her two little ones were infants and her husband was away on business. He laid Sofia on the changer, and, in short order, the baby was in a dry diaper and back in his arms.

Sofia cooed with contentment. He laughed at the sounds that reminded him of his nieces, then turned to find Natalie standing in the doorway of the nursery wearing a per-plexed look.

"Are you married with kids?" she asked.

He shook his head.

"Yet you know how to change diapers?"

"I've got two nieces, two years and eight months old. My sister said I was a quick study."

"She's right. I'm impressed."

Sofia jammed her tiny fist in her mouth and made sucking sounds.

"The baby's hungry." Everett rummaged in the tote and found a bottle of formula.

"Excuse me." He walked past Natalie into the main room where he settled into the couch.

"I'll feed Sofia while we have that talk you wanted." He glanced at the rifle she still held. "Can you park the weapon by the fireplace? Conversation flows better when I'm not star-ing at the end of a gun."

She hesitated.

"You can trust me, Natalie."

She shook her head and wrinkled her brow. "No, Everett, I can't. I can't trust anyone. Not you, not the other special agent who was with you tonight, and certainly not Mason Yates."

"Maybe we should skip the niceties and get right to what you want to talk about."

"I want to talk about a woman who fell

down the stairs to her death in Germany the way Tammy Yates died tonight."

Everett tensed. "Do you have a name?"

She nodded. "Paula Conway."

"And you think Mason Yates killed both women?"

"That's exactly what I think."

"Do you have proof?"

Her shoulders drooped. "I don't have anything except a gut feeling, which won't get me very far with law enforcement."

What had this woman been through that caused her to be so distrustful? Had Mason hurt her? If so, Everett would make sure he paid for his indiscretion or abuse.

Two women dying in the same way—if what Natalie said was true—raised more than a red flag. Everett didn't put much stock in hunches. Every person in law enforcement knew cases were solved with evidence, not subjective reactions or feelings, but something about Natalie Frazier tugged at his heart. She was nervous and afraid and appeared ready to collapse from the stress of what had happened.

"It's okay, Natalie." He wanted to reassure her. "I'm here to help you."

She nodded ever so slightly, then lowered

the gun to the floor and settled into a chair across from him.

His cell rang. Natalie tensed as he pulled it from his pocket. "Don't tell anyone where you are or that I'm with you," she warned.

He nodded. Seeing Frank's name, he swiped the call screen to establish a connection and then raised the cell to his ear. "This is Special Agent Kohl."

"Thanks for the tip about the apartment in Freemont. It's leased to Denise Lang, the nanny's roommate."

"You checked it out?"

Everett tried to appear nonchalant as Frank continued.

"Denise works the evening shift at a local restaurant and didn't show up tonight. The manager was worried and called the police."

"Okay."

"Almost simultaneously, we contacted them with questions about the nanny."

Everett glanced at Natalie. "And?"

"And once we arrived at the apartment, we realized we've got even bigger problems."

"Oh?"

"The local police found Denise Lang. She was murdered in her apartment."

Everett groaned. "How?"

"Cause of death was a bullet to the gut."

Everett listened as Frank told him who they suspected of committing the crime.

Disconnecting, he raised Sofia to his shoulder and leaned forward. "Tell me about Denise Lang."

"My roommate?"

"When did you last see her?"

"Yesterday before she went to work. She waitresses at a restaurant in Freemont."

"What about this morning?"

"She sleeps late. Her door was closed, and I didn't want to wake her. Why?"

"You stopped at your apartment tonight."

Natalie nodded. "She works nights and doesn't want anyone to call her while she's on the job. I left a note to tell her I would be out of touch for at least a day or so."

"The police checked your apartment to determine if you had anything to do with Tammy Yates's death."

Natalie slumped back in the chair. Color drained from her face. "They had no right."

"They had every right. Your roommate, Denise Lang, was found by the police."

She grimaced. "What?"

"Denise Lang was found dead. Two women died today, Tammy Yates and your roommate."

Natalie gasped. Her hand flew to her mouth, and her face twisted with grief.

"The police are searching for the killer." Everett pursed his lips, hoping she understood the seriousness of what he was about to say.

"The police are searching for you, Natalie. You're a person of interest."

Her blue eyes widened. "What's that mean?"

"It means they think you may have killed both women."

FOUR

A roar filled Natalie's ears. She grabbed the edge of the chair as the room shifted out of control, then hung her head to fend off the swell of nausea and light-headedness.

What she'd just heard couldn't be true.

"Are you okay?"

Everett's voice sounded garbled and distant, as if she were swimming underwater and couldn't make her way to the surface.

Denise? Gone?

His hand gripped her shoulder. "Take deep breaths. Keep your head down."

She gasped for air.

"You're pale as death, Natalie."

Bad choice of words. Her heart pounded even more. How could Denise be dead?

"Hold on." He left her side and hurried to the kitchen, where he ran water from the faucet and returned with a damp cloth that he placed on the back of her neck.

She fought to bring the world back into perspective and drew in a lungful of fresh air. Rubbing a hand over her still-queasy stomach, Natalie tried to make sense of what had happened, but nothing made sense. Not the fact that Mason Yates lived next to Wanda Davis or that his wife had been pushed to her death as Natalie listened to her scream for help.

She shivered, unable to wipe the horrific scene from her mind. The vision shifted, and, instead of Tammy lying dead at the foot of the stairs, she saw Denise.

"No," she moaned, and rubbed her forehead. "I...I can't believe—"

"Shh." His hand stroked her shoulder. "Relax for a few minutes. There'll be time to talk later."

Time to talk when he hauled her back to Fort Rickman. Tears burned her eyes and a huge lump filled her throat. Even drawing a shallow breath took effort.

The swirl of confusion played havoc with her emotions. She should have moved back to Detroit. The inner-city blight would have been easier to handle than what was happening in Georgia.

All she wanted was to get a job in education and earn enough to live life without drawing attention to herself or her past. The warmth of a small town, Freemont, with its strong sense of community and welcoming arms, had seemed an ideal location in which to sink roots and perhaps, someday, find someone special and raise a family.

That dream for her future was out of the question now. The way things looked, she didn't even have a future.

A person of interest in the deaths of two women?

She groaned.

"It's okay, Natalie."

Special Agent Kohl was either terribly confused or too much of an optimist. Nothing was okay. All she saw was darkness and heartache.

Somehow she had to clear her name, but so much was stacked against her. Everett was a special agent on the hunt for a killer. A bull's-eye was painted on her back, and in spite of his seeming concern for her present well-being, he couldn't change the mind-set of the powers that be at Fort Rickman.

With Mason spouting lies about what had happened in Germany, the CID would come to the wrong conclusion. She didn't have a chance, unless she could uncover evidence that proved Mason's guilt and convince Everett of her innocence. Would the special agent be a help or a hindrance?

Everett hated being the bearer of bad news, and Natalie appeared to have had her quota today. He'd never seen anyone blanch so quickly or look so fragile.

Criminals were habitually good actors, but the total shock Natalie seemed to be experiencing was hard to feign. Still, he needed to be cautious.

He placed the baby in the crib. By the time he had retraced his steps, Natalie's breathing was more even, and her deathly pallor had changed to a healthier hue.

He filled a glass with water and added ice.

"How 'bout a drink?" he offered.

"Thanks." She reached for the glass. "I...I can't believe—"

Her voice caught. She turned away from his gaze and shook her head. "Denise? It can't be true."

"How long had you known her?"

"Almost a year. She needed a roommate and placed an ad in the Freemont paper. I responded and moved in the following day."

"You were good friends?"

Natalie took a sip of water and shrugged. "We shared an apartment. Denise worked nights, and I was gone most days to my classes. On the weekends, we each went our separate way."

"Was there anyone who wanted to do her harm?"

"Not that I know of, although she'd been dating a guy for about two months. Their relationship was questionable in my mind."

"In what way?"

"He wanted everything kept private. She wouldn't even tell me his name." Natalie glanced up, her expression open and unassuming. "I thought that was strange and not what I would want in a relationship."

"Did she know how you felt?"

"I'd mentioned the importance of trust. She wasn't one to take advice."

"So you knew nothing about him?"

"Only that they met outside of town, and he never came to our apartment."

"Any chance he could have been married?"

"That's what I thought, which upset me. Denise was a good person. She came from a great family. I couldn't understand why she would keep the guy's identity secret."

Natalie took another sip of water before continuing. "Whatever was going on affected Denise. She had changed over the last few weeks. She used to be upbeat and happy. Recently, she'd seemed on edge."

"Did she reveal anything about the boyfriend?"

"Only that he drove fast cars."

"More than one?"

"She mentioned a sports car and a sedan." Natalie's eyes widened. "How many cars does Mason drive?"

Everett didn't see that coming. "Why do you think he might be the boyfriend?"

"I'm just searching for a common thread between the two deaths."

A common thread that didn't involve her.

Everett pulled his cell from his pocket. "I'll call post and pass the information on to Frank."

Natalie grabbed his hand. "Please don't. The CID will want me to return to post. I'm afraid of what Mason might do."

"I won't let anyone hurt you."

She bit her lip. "Mason's opinion will carry weight. He could make up all sorts of stories about our time in Vilseck, all of which would paint me in a bad light. I don't trust him, and the CID will be more prone to believe one of their own than anything I have to say."

Natalie was right about Mason's statements carrying weight. She was an unknown. He was an established investigator.

Her mention of Germany raised another red flag. "Mason was your supervisor in Vilseck. Did he threaten you?"

Her shoulders slumped ever so slightly. "He…he had a wandering eye." Her voice was barely a whisper.

Everett fisted his hands in respond to the flash of anger that swept over him. "Did anything happen?"

"I was careful to keep my distance."

"Did you issue a sexual harassment complaint?"

"That would have made the situation worse."

Natalie should have issued a complaint that would have been investigated. Instead, she'd reacted like too many women and remained silent for fear of retribution. Everett didn't understand her logic, but then he'd never been in such a situation.

"Do you have any proof of his inappropriate actions?"

She shook her head. "He was careful to insure no one heard his comments."

Everett let out a stiff breath. "So you didn't issue a complaint because it would have been your word against his."

"Exactly. I was due to return to the States and decided not to reenlist. Freemont is a nice town. I thought I could start fresh there, never thinking I'd see Mason again. That's why I can't go back to Fort Rickman. He'll bring up Germany, only he'll twist what happened and make it seem that I was the one at fault."

"You're jumping to the wrong conclusion."

"Am I?" She tugged at her hair. "After I left, rumors circulated to that effect. One of the other personnel clerks emailed me and told me what she had heard."

"Did she know where the rumors had originated?"

"She didn't need to tell me. I knew. Mason spread lies about me to make sure his name wasn't sullied."

The sincerity in her voice and the strength of her conviction brought back memories of another woman who had been threatened by a superior. Everett hadn't looked deep enough into that case, and the results had been catastrophic. He couldn't make the same mistake again.

The lines of fatigue around Natalie's eyes were telling. She was exhausted and needed rest.

"Let's wait until morning," he suggested. "Then we can decide what to do next."

She flicked her gaze around the cabin and nervously tugged at the sleeve of her sweater. "I'm not going back to Fort Rickman."

"We'll decide in the morning."

"You don't believe me, that's why you're determined to take me in."

"I have a job to do, Natalie."

"You have a job to find out the truth. That's what you told me earlier. I didn't kill Denise, and I had nothing to do with Tammy Yates's death."

"Two deaths in one day are more than a coincidence. You seem to be the common denominator."

"That doesn't make me a killer."

She was right, but it did make her a possible suspect. Everett should be in his car driving her back to the CID Headquarters at Fort Rickman or to the Freemont police. Both law enforcement agencies considered her a person of interest. Everett did, as well, but ever since Specialist Carolyn Rogers had stepped into his cubicle seven years ago, he'd been overly cautious about jumping to the wrong conclusions, which is why he was hesitant to take Natalie back to post, at least not tonight.

Eventually she would need to be questioned by law enforcement, but right now, he was concerned about Mason Yates and the strings he might pull to wrap the investigation up too quickly. Getting to the truth was the bottom line. Natalie wasn't a threat or a flight risk tonight. By morning, the CID might have more information that would shed light on both crimes.

Hopefully, Natalie's innocence would be established. If not, Everett would have to admit his mistake. The delay might cost him his career, but he had to trust himself and everything inside him told him to be cautious.

How could he look at himself in the mirror, even if his career advanced, if an innocent woman's life was ruined in the process? He had to follow his gut on this one.

Was she guilty or innocent? A hard question he couldn't answer. At least not yet.

FIVE

Once Natalie had turned in, Everett stepped outside and slowly walked around the cabin. He had followed Natalie here from Fort Rickman, which meant someone else could have, as well. Like the killer who had thrown Tammy Yates to her death or whoever had shot Denise Lang.

The moon broke through the dark cloud cover. In the distance, he could see a lake and boat dock. The scene looked peaceful, but anything—or anyone—could be lurking in the shadows.

Slowly, he approached Natalie's car and spied the keys in the ignition. Opening the door, he hesitated for a long moment as a floral scent, like the gardenias his mom grew in her garden, wafted past him. He had noticed the scent earlier when he'd stood close to Natalie, but now it brought thoughts of a determined woman who wanted to keep baby Sofia safe. Natalie tried to appear tough, yet the totally feminine scent she wore and her concern for the infant revealed something about the real person beneath the facade.

Everett admired her spunk and focus. She was pretty with her black hair and big eyes that stirred an awareness deep within him. The intensity of her gaze haunted him. She seemed to plead for help yet refused to ask, as if any sign of weakness should be kept hidden.

Checking his watch, he did the math with the six-hour time difference between Georgia and Germany, then punched in a number and waited until Special Agent Tyler Zimmerman answered.

"Hey, buddy, it's Everett. I heard you were in Vilseck."

"Good to hear your voice, Rett. Last I knew you were at Fort Sill."

"And transferred to Rickman some months ago."

"A good assignment," Tyler said, "if you're working for Craig Wilson."

Surprised by the comment, Everett asked, "You know Wilson?"

"Only by reputation. Do me a favor, and put in a plug for me."

"How long before you PCS back to the States?"

"I spent two-and-a-half years at Heidelberg, and the last eight months here in Vilseck. I could ask for a transfer in a couple more months, especially if Wilson requests me. Tell the chief that I'm an outstanding special agent with exceptional investigative skills."

Everett chuckled. "I'll let him know."

"Appreciate the support, but you didn't call to talk about my career goals. What's up?"

Everett cut to the chase. "Special Agent Mason Yates's wife died a few hours ago. She either fell or was pushed down the stars in their quarters."

Tyler let out a stiff breath. "That's tough. How's Mason?"

"Grieving, of course. He wasn't home at the time of death. Right now we don't have any leads." At least none Everett wanted to reveal. "A personnel clerk, Specialist Natalie Frazier, worked with the CID and left Vilseck about a year ago. I need information on her and any involvement she might have had with Mason."

"Involvement? You mean a relationship?"

"Supposedly not, but let me know if any

scuttlebutt is floating around. I don't put stock in rumors, although sometimes they hold a hint of truth."

"I'll be discreet."

"There's something else. A woman fell down the stairs to her death in Vilseck while Mason was there. Her name was Paula Conway. See if anyone remembers the incident. Let me know what you uncover."

"Roger that."

After disconnecting, Everett stared into the woods. The chatter of cicadas and tree frogs filled the night. Returning the cell to his ear, he made one more call, this time to bring Frank Gallagher up-to-date.

"You need to drive Natalie Frazier back to Fort Rickman. If not now, then in the morning," Frank insisted once Everett explained the situation.

"I'll talk to her and get back to you, but I have to tell you, Frank, she's been forthright about everything so far."

"She can be forthright at Fort Rickman."

Everett told him about the roommate's boyfriend. "See if you can find out who Denise was seeing. Could be a married man who wants to keep his transgressions quiet."

"I'll pass that on to the Freemont police."

"Although it's a long shot, we need to be certain Mason isn't involved."

Frank's sharp inhale sounded over the phone. "Did Natalie think he was seeing her roommate?"

"It's purely speculation, although wouldn't that be an interesting twist?"

"One I don't like."

"I don't, either, but that doesn't mean we don't follow every lead. Plus, Natalie had two prank phone calls on the Joneses' landline earlier tonight. Check Mason's cell, just in case."

Frank sniffed. "You're treading on thin ice, Rett. Mason's record is squeaky clean. The unknown in this situation is the nanny. Easy enough for her to concoct a story in order to shift blame to someone else. Someone who could end up being Chief of Fort Rickman CID, if Wilson transfers."

"I'm the one suggesting the connection, Frank. You can blame me."

He and Frank both knew they were walking on a slippery slope that could have them tumbling downward in a heartbeat, especially if Mason stepped into Wilson's shoes.

"I'll check Mason's cell and make inquiries about the roommate's boyfriend," Frank said before he disconnected. "Call me in the morning."

Everett pocketed his phone with a sigh. Natalie had opened up tonight. Surely she would reveal more information in the morning. Once Everett heard back from Tyler, he'd know a bit more about what had happened in Germany.

After stepping back into the cabin, he locked the door behind him and stood in the dark room. For a long moment, he stared through the picture window at the lake in the distance. In spite of the placid water and serenity of the night, Everett couldn't calm his unrest. Too many questions needed to be answered.

Glancing at his watch, he sighed. Morning would come soon enough. Settling onto the couch, he rested his head on the cushions and closed his eyes.

Frank wanted Natalie hauled back to CID Headquarters, but Everett had made a vow long ago never to leave any question unanswered in future investigations. He'd keep Natalie under surveillance and close at hand until he had a clear picture of what had happened at the Yateses' duplex on post and Denise Lang's apartment in Freemont. Two women. Two murders. Both needed to be solved.

Tired as Natalie was, the memory of Tammy Yates's body lying at the bottom of the stairs circled through her dreams. She'd tossed and turned for a period of time, and after finally falling into a deep sleep, she startled awake just before dawn. Everett had encouraged her to use the master bedroom, but she'd assured him the single bed in the baby's room was more than comfortable. Plus, she wanted to hear Sofia if the little one stirred in the night.

The infant wasn't the one thrashing around in the dark. Sounds from the main living area filtered through the closed door to the nursery. Natalie wondered if the special agent was struggling with his own bad dreams.

Tiptoeing from her bed, she cracked open the door and stared into the darkness, hearing a rhythmic vibration. Unable to discern the origin of the noise, she padded softly across the hardwood floor to the couch.

Everett lay sprawled along the rather narrow cushions with his head cocked at what appeared to be an uncomfortable angle. His long legs hung over the edge of the couch. That the man could even sleep was a testament to his fatigue.

The vibration sounded again, drawing Natalie's attention to the mobile cell on the coffee table. Bending down, she read Frank Gallagher's name on the lit screen.

Earlier, Natalie hadn't wanted Everett to phone his buddy in the CID, but she couldn't let a call go unanswered that might provide encouraging news about the investigation.

She touched Everett's arm.

He jerked awake. His brow wrinkled, and his eyes widened. With one swift motion, he sat up and reached for the phone. "Special Agent Everett Kohl."

Natalie straightened her sweater and tugged at her jeans. Knowing dawn would come too soon, she'd slept in her clothes, which Everett had done, too.

He scrubbed his left hand over his face. "What time will Lieutenant Jones's flight arrive at Hartsfield?"

The Atlanta airport. Wanda must have made a reservation.

Everett glanced up. Even in the darkness, Natalie could see the concern in his gaze.

"Roger that," he said into the phone. "I'll talk to her and let you know." He disconnected.

Leaning closer, Natalie raised her brow. "Didn't we have a deal that you wouldn't mention being with me until morning?"

He pointed to the pinkish glow streaming through the window. "There's light on the horizon. I call that morning, and we never had a deal. I said we would decide what to do after we both got some rest." He glanced at his watch. "You caught an hour and a half of shut-eye. Not enough, but it'll have to suffice."

Letting out a deep breath, Everett stood, looking tall and muscular and so very male. She took a step back and straightened her spine, unwilling to let down her guard.

"Did you tell Frank about this cabin?" she asked.

Everett nodded. "I called him after you went to sleep last night."

"What?" She wanted to stamp her foot and spout off a list of terms that would ease her frustration, but she'd left that part of her life behind in Detroit and was a better and more civil person these days. Instead, she glared at him.

"Evidently—" she kept her voice low but firm "—I can't believe a word you say."

"For your information, Chief Agent-in-Charge Craig Wilson heads the CID at Fort Rickman. He's out of town, and Frank is in charge. I had to inform him about your whereabouts, Natalie. I also told him about the prank phone calls and Denise's clandestine relationship with the nameless boyfriend. He notified the Freemont police and both agencies are investigating."

"Did you say Mason could be the boyfriend?"

Everett nodded. "I mentioned that as a long shot, but one that needed to be on the table."

"But he still thinks I'm the killer?"

Everett pursed his lips. "He considers you a person of interest."

She turned from him and hugged herself, unwilling to give in to the tears that stung her eyes. No one believed her.

"I'm not going to desert you, Natalie. Getting answers is key to this investigation right now. That, and reuniting Sofia with her mother."

"I can't go back to Fort Rickman. Not while Mason's there."

Everett sighed. "I understand your concern, but that doesn't change the fact that the baby needs her mother, although I'm not sure where we should meet."

"Wanda drove to the airport and left her car in long-term parking. She took a shuttle to the terminal. Meeting at the airport would be so public." Her stomach twisted at the thought. "A better plan might be to connect in the parking lot. What time does her plane land?"

"She's scheduled to arrive at noon."

Natalie reached for her cell. "Then I should be able to reach her." She pulled up Wanda's name on her phone directory and tapped the listing.

The cell rang when she lifted it to her ear.

"How's my baby?" Wanda answered.

"Sofia's fine. She's sleeping soundly. We're at your cabin."

Natalie hesitated, thinking of Denise and what had happened. Unwilling to share more bad news with Wanda, she didn't mention her roommate.

"My plane arrives at noon," Wanda informed her, confirming the flight details Frank had provided. They made arrangements to meet at the long-term parking lot in Atlanta where Wanda's car was parked before disconnecting the call.

Natalie turned back to Everett. "I'd feel safer if we left the cabin now. If Frank knows I'm here, he might share the information with Mason."

"How's coffee sound?"

"Like just what I need."

"I passed a diner on the way here last night. Let's get some chow before we head to Atlanta."

"Sofia will be safe with us, won't she?" Natalie needed reassurance.

Everett's eyes showed his concern. "I won't let anything happen to either of you."

Natalie wished with all her heart that she could believe him. But it was her responsibility to make certain nothing stopped Sofia from reuniting with her mother. Once they were together, then Natalie could focus on her own safety—and how to uncover the truth about the two women who had been murdered.

SIX

Everett pointed to the nursery. "Get the baby ready while I move your car closer to the cabin. We'll return for it later."

"On our way back to Fort Rickman?" Natalie's voice held a sharp edge.

"You mentioned college courses to get your teaching certificate. You can't walk away from your future."

"In case you haven't noticed, my future is in shambles right now. Find out the truth about Mason, and then I'll return to post."

Everett slowly nodded. "Okay. Any suggestions on how to get to the truth?"

His question must have given her pause. She lowered herself onto the couch and stared at him for a long moment. "Contact the CID office in Vilseck. Ask them to give you all they have on Paula Conway."

He slipped into the chair across from her

and pulled out his notebook and pen. "I need more details."

"Mason and his wife lived on the economy."

"Not on the military *kaserne*? You mean they rented a German house?"

"That's right. An apartment in one of the small towns around Vilseck near where Paula lived. She was a teacher in the Department of Defense School and worked with Tammy."

Natalie took a deep breath before she continued. "Paula was a single mom with two children. The kids were at an all-night activity at the teen center on the *kaserne*. When she failed to pick them up in the morning, the youth director called Tammy and asked her to check on the missing mom."

"The youth director didn't ask to speak to Mason?"

"According to the story I heard, Paula had left Tammy's name as an emergency contact. Mason was working at the office that Saturday and not at home."

"What did Tammy find?" Everett tensed, too aware of how the story would end.

"Paula was dead." Natalie's eyes clouded. "She had fallen down the stairs in her apartment."

Just like Tammy Yates's death. "She's the woman you mentioned last night."

"That's right." Natalie glanced down before she spoke. "I told you Mason had spread rumors after I left Vilseck. I didn't want his lies to follow me back to the States."

"Was there an investigation?"

"Yes, but it was handled by the German *polizei*."

"Not the CID?"

"Paula lived in German housing so the local police took the case. They determined that her death was accidental."

"Wouldn't the military get involved?"

Natalie stared at him with serious eyes. "Remember who was in charge of the CID office at that time."

"You're saying Mason made the decision to go with the German police assessment?"

"That's right. Why waste man-hours and personnel on a death that was accidental? At least, that's the reasoning he used."

"You worked for him at that time?"

She nodded.

"Did you state your concerns to Mason or to anyone else?"

"I didn't feel qualified. I was just a personnel clerk and not law enforcement. At the time, I didn't know about Mason's wandering eye. Nor had I heard the whispers about the time he and Paula had been seen together at a *gasthaus* in a neighboring town. The ugliness surfaced later."

"By *gasthaus*, do you mean a restaurant or an inn?"

"This one had both. Mason and Paula could have been having lunch, although some folks thought more was going on."

Everett rubbed his hand over his face. Why hadn't Natalie been forthcoming about Mason's dalliances the first time he questioned her? Just as Frank had mentioned, she could be making up a story to build her own case against her former boss.

"You said Mason came on to you. Now you claim he was involved with a schoolteacher? Which is it?"

She let out a frustrated breath. "You wanted information, which I'm providing. I don't have proof of his relationship with Paula. I'm just passing on what I heard. Mason and Tammy socialized with her. In fact, Paula had dinner at the Yateses' home the night she died."

Another interesting detail. "If something was going on, Mason's wife must have been unaware of the situation."

"I'm not sure who knew what or if the rumors were valid. As I mentioned, Mason has spread some malicious lies about me. Wagging tongues can cause great damage to people's lives. I wouldn't be telling you this if I didn't feel you needed to know."

The tone of her voice made Everett realize there were other details she wanted to share, if only he could ask the right questions.

Sitting back in the chair, he hesitated before asking, "Why don't you tell me how Mason hurt you?"

Natalie hadn't expected Everett's comment to strike a nerve. Perhaps it was the sincerity of his voice or the understanding she saw in his eyes or perhaps her own fatigue and fear that added to her vulnerability and desire to get everything out in the open. Once Everett heard what had happened in Germany, he might understand why she was so worried about Mason. But where to start?

She pulled in a deep breath. "A few weeks after Paula's death, Mason began making inappropriate comments around me. I ignored them at first and gave him the benefit of the doubt, thinking he didn't realize what he was saying. I wondered if I was overreacting and making more of his statements than I should have. Especially since he was the head of the CID office."

"And those subtle and not-so-subtle comments continued for some time?"

She nodded, remembering her upset as Mason continued to taunt her. "I tried to ignore him, but that was difficult, to say the least. When things got too intense, I'd leave work, claiming I had an appointment or needed to see my company commander. As I mentioned earlier, he never said anything questionable when others could hear him."

"Did he get the message?"

"I think it made him mad. He started following me after work. I was afraid to go home. Sometimes I'd drive through the German countryside to elude him."

"But he must have had access to your address and knew where you lived."

"My name and address were on the duty roster so, of course, he knew. A few times, I noticed a sedan parked outside my apartment. He drove a midsize four-door sedan at that time. I'm not sure of the exact make or model. If I saw his car, I'd keep the lights off and hoped he thought I wasn't home."

"Maybe it was another guy who was interested in you, someone you had dated?"

She shook her head. "I...I didn't have time to date. I was taking college courses online that required extensive reading. My days were full between work and school."

"Except you had the added worry of Mason."

"That's it exactly." Maybe Everett did understand how she had felt. "Mason asked me to work late a number of times. I told him I couldn't. One Sunday, he called and requested a certain file from the office. I made up an excuse. He became angry and said I needed to remember that he was the boss and insinuated he'd bring me up on some type of charge."

"You should have registered a grievance."

"I realize that now." She glanced out the window, thinking of that dark time in her life that had overpowered her in Germany.

"Mason's threats became more insistent," she continued. "He'd phone in the middle of the night and hang up when I answered. At two different times, my tires were slashed. The *polizei* blamed it on vandals, but Mason always made a comment the next day at work that made me know he was involved. His taunts turned to threats. He said he'd make me regret rejecting him."

She bit her lip and hesitated for a long moment, trying to find the words to explain her actions. "You probably think I was foolish not to have taken action against him, but it's the way I had always reacted to problems. I packed my bag and left Detroit to get away from my overcontrolling mom and my bad home life. In my mind, it was safer to run away than to confront a difficult situation."

She raked her hand through her hair and sighed. "Plus, I…I didn't want anything negative on my military record, and I knew Mason could have hurt me both physically and militarily. The only way to guarantee my good name and my safety was to leave Germany and the military. At the time, I thought I was making the right decision."

"You transferred back to the States and put in your paperwork to transition out of the military?"

"That's right."

"But you ended up at the same post to which Mason was eventually transferred." Everett pursed his lips before he continued. "Some might think it was prearranged."

The statement cut into her heart. She had shared the information with Everett to make him aware of who Mason really was.

Steeling her spine, she stood. "You can see

it however you want, Everett, but I'm telling the truth."

Sofia's cry sounded from the nursery. Glad for a reason to escape the CID agent's penetrating gaze, Natalie hurried to the bedroom and lifted the baby into her arms. As much as she wanted to soothe the infant, she also wanted to console her own troubled heart. Why wouldn't Everett believe her and see Mason for who he really was?

Everett strode outside, trying to make sense of what Natalie had said. She seemed sincere, but, as much as he wanted to believe her, he needed evidence to substantiate her accusations against Mason.

Frustrated by his own inability to sort out the truth, he grabbed Natalie's suitcases and the baby's extra tote from her car and placed them in the rear of his SUV. Then he switched Sofia's car seat for the trip to Atlanta.

Once the baby's seat was securely installed, he moved both cars and parked his SUV in front of the cabin. His steps were heavy as he climbed the stairs to the porch. Opening the front door, he stopped short.

Natalie sat on the couch with the baby in her

arms. Sofia hungrily sucked from a bottle. Her small hand clasped Natalie's finger.

Not wanting to disrupt the serenity of the moment, he stood staring at the two of them as Natalie smiled down at the baby. The concern that had lined her face earlier had been replaced with a sweet joy that tugged at his heart. For too long, he'd ignored an inner yearning to have a woman in his life. This morning, the emptiness he had refused to acknowledge seemed all too real.

His parents were happily married. He'd grown up thinking he'd eventually find someone special. There had been one girl, but she wasn't interested in a long-distance relationship nor the nomadic military life. After that he focused on his job and never allowed time for anything outside of the military.

Why would he feel a surge of longing now in the middle of an investigation? Even more disconcerting was his attraction toward the one person who had a very real connection to not only Tammy Yates's death but also Denise Lang's murder.

Everett had made a mistake once. He couldn't accept or discard the information Natalie had provided without substantiating her statements.

He had to find out the truth about Natalie.

He needed to find out the truth about Mason, also. Both their futures hung in the balance.

She glanced up, as if just realizing he was staring at her. The need for acceptance flashed from her eyes before she turned her gaze once again to the baby.

Hoping to bring his full attention back to the investigation, Everett wiped his feet on the entryway rug and closed the door behind him.

"Almost ready?" he asked a bit too briskly.

Natalie lifted the baby to her shoulder. "Sofia needs to be burped, then I'll grab her things."

"Stay where you are. I'll get them."

"Is something wrong?" She stared at him as he crossed the room to the nursery.

She must have heard the harshness in his voice. Instead of keeping his internal turmoil in check, he'd made his own frustration evident in the sharpness of his tone. Natalie didn't deserve his gruffness.

"I'm just eager to get going."

He couldn't tell her about the mixed emotions that only served to pull him off task and away from the investigation to something much more personal. All too aware that Natalie's nearness was playing havoc with his common sense, he entered the baby's room and quickly placed Sofia's things back in the diaper bag. Glancing into the living room, he watched Natalie carry the baby to the window and stare out into the gray dawn.

As if again feeling his gaze, she turned to stare at him, her eyes filled with question.

Grabbing the diaper bag, he returned to the living area and pointed to the door. "Let's get going."

She moved away from the window. Before she'd taken three steps, the crack of a gunshot sounded in the early-morning stillness.

The window shattered. Shards of glass flew like shrapnel through the air.

In one swoop, Everett covered Natalie and the infant with his body and pulled them to the floor.

She screamed. The baby cried.

He drew his weapon. "Stay down."

Crawling to the window, he peered over the edge of the sill and searched for movement. Hampered by the faint morning light, he hurried back to her side. "I'll check the grounds."

"Be careful, Everett."

He squeezed her hand and slipped out the kitchen door. Staying close to the side of the cabin, he stared at the expansive lawn and the lake beyond, then slowly and methodically, he circled the building, his eyes on the forest that edged the property. Every few steps, he stopped, narrowed his gaze and searched for anything out of the norm that would indicate a person hiding in the underbrush.

Even though he saw no one, the shooter could still be hiding nearby. Everett returned to the cabin and motioned Natalie, with the baby in her arms, toward the door.

"We've got to get out of here. I'll step onto the porch first. Stay back until I signal you."

She nodded and cradled Sofia close to her heart.

Everett inched open the cabin's front door and stared at the gravel drive and surrounding tree cover. The shooter could be anywhere.

He pulled in a deep breath and counted to ten before he stepped onto the porch, gun raised and at the ready.

Turning his ear, he listened for any sound that might indicate movement. A squirrel scampered up a tree. Overhead, a crow cawed.

Moving swiftly, he opened the car's rear door and waved Natalie forward. Then he stood guard with his gun extended while she and the baby raced from the cabin and climbed into the backseat of the SUV. She clicked the baby into the car seat and adjusted her own seat belt.

"No one's following us," Everett said as they left the gravel driveway and turned onto the narrow country road.

"It was Mason," she insisted. "Frank told him where to find me."

Everett had instructed Frank to keep information from the senior CID agent. Had he ignored the advice?

A heavy weight settled on his shoulders. If Natalie was telling the truth about Germany, then the shooter at the cabin could be the person who had killed Tammy Yates and Denise Lang. Just as Natalie had said, that person could be Mason.

SEVEN

Natalie's pulse throbbed, and her heart pounded at breakneck speed as the countryside flew past them. Everett's gaze flicked between the road ahead and the rearview mirror. His hands gripped the steering wheel white-knuckled, which made her all too aware of the gravity of the situation. They were exposed and vulnerable.

Again, she glanced over her shoulder at the long stretch of empty roadway behind them. The rising sun hovered low on the horizon and bathed the world in a soft glow that should have brought comfort; instead, she felt a chilling need to run away from whatever and whoever was following them.

Could Denise's boyfriend be the assailant? Would he have killed Denise and then driven to post to kill Tammy Yates? If so, what would be his motive?

Her insides turned to jelly as realization hit. There was only one way to explain both deaths. Natalie had thought of it before, but now she was even surer of the man tied to both crimes.

Mason!

Everything led back to him.

She shivered, not from the cold, but from fear that she would never be free from his evil manipulation.

"No one's on our tail," Everett assured her from the front of the car, as if he recognized her inner struggle.

"Maybe he followed you from post." Natalie gave voice to a likely explanation of how Mason had tracked her down.

Another thought came to her.

What if the two CID agents were working together and Everett knew Mason was lying in wait until the perfect moment to strike.

She'd awakened once and heard something outside the cabin. Pulling back the curtain, she'd seen Everett staring at the lake. Had he left the house to talk to Mason and plan the morning strike?

Only one bullet had fired, and thankfully both she and the baby had stepped away from the window and the flying shards of glass in time. If the gunshot had been to scare her instead of doing harm, Mason could be playing with her, trying to assert his dominance and control.

Her hands trembled as she tucked a strand of hair behind her ear and stared at Everett. If only she could sort through the confusion that surrounded her. Right now, she wasn't sure of anything except that someone was after her. Glancing down at Sofia, asleep in her car seat, a swell of determination and resolve filled her.

Whatever happened, she had to protect this precious little one from Mason, from Denise's killer, and even from Everett, if need be. Bottom line, when it came to Sofia's safety, she could trust no one.

Gazing out the window at the passing landscape, Natalie remembered words of scripture she'd heard from a street-corner preacher who had tried to bring faith to the chaos of her Detroit neighborhood.

I can do all things through Christ who strengthens me.

If only she could.

Everett's worst nightmare had come true. Someone had fired a shot through the cabin window that could have struck Natalie and the baby. He hadn't been vigilant enough to realize the danger. Instead, he'd slipped into a complacency that had almost gotten Natalie killed.

Needing to relay the information to the CID at Fort Rickman, he reached for his cell and punched Frank's number. His longtime buddy answered on the second ring, sounding groggy with sleep.

"Morning, sunshine. Sorry I woke you."

"What's up, Rett?"

"Someone fired a shot through the cabin window this morning."

"Anyone hurt?"

"Negative. We're on the road, heading to Atlanta. So far no one's following us."

"Did you see the shooter?"

"No sign of him at all."

"Strange, eh?"

"You've got that right." Everett glanced at Natalie in the rearview mirror. Her eyes were wide, her face drawn. "Did you tell Mason where Natalie was staying?"

"Of course not. You wanted me to keep that close hold, which I did. Even if you hadn't mentioned your concern, I wouldn't have provided the information. Mason's doing everything right, but he's still the husband in what could be a domestic-violence death. I'm not sharing anything with him. Is that understood?"

"Glad we're both on the same page. He needs to be questioned, and keep your eye on him. Check that he's at the Lodge and hasn't been wandering around a certain fishing cabin."

"You think he fired the shot?"

"Just locate him, Frank. Make sure he's where he said he would be. Might be wise to question him again concerning Germany and his relationship with Natalie Frazier."

"Was there a relationship?"

"Not on her part."

"You're saying Mason was interested?"

Everett hesitated, choosing his words. "I'm saying find out his take on the situation. I've got a call in to a friend who works in the Vilseck CID office. Let's find out as much as we can and then compare notes."

"Roger that."

"Do me a favor and alert the local sheriff's office about the shooting. Could have been some hunter whose aim was off, but I doubt it. Just notify the local authorities and see if they come across anything."

"Will do."

"What about Denise Lang's murder? Have the Freemont police provided any new information?"

"Not yet. They're supposed to call me if anything breaks. Last I heard they were trying to track down the boyfriend."

"You told them the two deaths could be related."

"I did. What about Natalie Frazier? Anything new I should know?"

Again, Everett glanced at her in the rear. She was smiling at Sofia, which made his chest tighten. "Nothing new. Just keep your eye on Mason. He needs to remain on post. I don't want him or anyone else following us to Atlanta, is that understood?"

"Mason scheduled a meeting with the chaplain today to plan his wife's funeral. I doubt he'll be leaving post."

"Is the autopsy report back?"

"Not yet."

"And the video footage from the track?"

"Evidently the cameras haven't worked for weeks."

"So we can't establish Mason was running in the training area."

"He says another guy saw him. He was wearing a Second of the Fifth Infantry T-shirt.

We're checking the unit to see if anyone comes forward to verify Mason's alibi."

"Sounds like a needle in a haystack."

"Maybe, but we might get lucky."

"What about the MPs who went door-to-door in the Yateses' housing area? Did they learn anything from the neighbors?"

"No one saw anything, except that lieutenant who talked to you last night. He lives across the street."

"Lieutenant Bobby Slade?"

"That's him. He noticed a strange car parked behind the Yateses' quarters in the afternoon just as you mentioned, but he can't provide details. Of course, he wants answers for everything else like four hours ago. Although I don't blame the guy. He's worried about his wife being in danger. Evidently he's going TDY in the next few days to Fort Drum and doesn't like leaving her alone with a killer on the loose."

"Let's hope we can wrap this investigation up by then."

"Exactly. The chief returns next week. I'd like everything to have calmed down by the time he comes back to post."

"We'll make it happen, Frank."

Everett disconnected and returned his phone

to the console. The first forty-eight hours in an investigation were the most crucial. Right now, the CID and Freemont police both seemed to be striking out.

If only something would break soon.

Natalie didn't share Everett's optimism about the case. From the one-sided conversation she had overheard, he hoped to have everything wrapped up in a short time. Who was he trying to fool? If Mason were allowed to go free, his wife's death would never be solved.

Supposedly the Freemont police were looking into Denise's murder, but the last Natalie had heard was that they thought she was involved. If only they could find the elusive boyfriend.

Again, she tried to piece the parts together to end up with some logical explanation about what had happened. Everything pointed to Mason, yet he remained at large.

She looked over her shoulder as Everett made two quick turns. "Where are we going?" she asked, suddenly concerned about the back roads she didn't recognize.

"Eventually to the highway. I'm taking a circuitous route to the interstate north of here."

Thick forest spread out on each side of the

road and made her anxious. Glancing down at the baby, asleep in the car seat, brought a wave of sadness.

Lord, I haven't prayed for years, but I'm concerned about this sweet baby. Keep her safe.

Keep me safe, too.

"You okay?" Everett stared at her from the rearview mirror.

She might as well be forthright about her concerns. "I'm trying to decide if you led someone to me."

He let out a stiff breath and shook his head, as if frustrated by her statement. "No one followed me, Natalie."

"Then how did he find me?"

"You're convinced it was Mason?"

She glanced out the window and into the shadowed recesses of the wooded landscape.

"The two deaths could be coincidental," he added when she failed to respond. "They may not be related."

"Since when did someone in law enforcement put stock in coincidence? From everything I've read, seen on television or heard when working with the CID, there are no coincidences. If things seem random, they're not. Any patterns need to be recognized as significant." She stared at the back of Everett's head. "Isn't that true?"

"Things can be coincidental, but it's often a red flag that needs to be investigated."

She nodded. "A red flag. That's how I feel about the shooter in the woods. That's why I think you led him to me. I'm not sure if it was planned or accidental."

"I'm not the bad guy." He stared at her in the mirror for a long moment. Then he shrugged and returned his gaze to the road. "Everything will work out. We'll meet Wanda and reunite Sofia with her mother."

"And then?"

He glanced back at her. "Then I'll let you decide where you want to go."

Not back to Fort Rickman, which she'd already mentioned.

"You heard me mention a CID buddy who transferred to Vilseck some months ago," Everett continued. "I asked him to reopen Paula Conway's stairway death case."

"But I told you the German police handled the investigation."

"I know. The CID will contact them and ask for any evidence they gathered. The *polizei* may or may not have interviewed neighbors. There could have been witnesses."

"What about Mason's neighbors in the housing area at Fort Rickman? You said he might not have been home when his wife died. Does he have an alibi?"

"MPs went door-to-door. One neighbor saw a car parked behind the Yateses' quarters, but he didn't know the make or model. Mason claimed to have been running on the track in the training area."

"Were there video cameras?"

"They weren't working."

She huffed. "Well, that's convenient."

"Investigations require a lot of tedious checking and rechecking. Some leads pan out. Others don't."

"You're telling me to be patient."

"I'm trying to explain that Frank is on top of the investigation. He'll check every clue and won't leave any shred of evidence uncovered."

Although she was somewhat relieved that Paula's death was being reviewed, Natalie wasn't optimistic about the outcome. Memories clouded with time, and she doubted the CID would uncover anything that would incriminate Mason.

Everett glanced at the rearview mirror, but his gaze wasn't on her this time. It was on the road behind them.

She turned, seeing headlights. "We're being followed."

"Keep your head down."

They crested a small hill, and on the downward side, Everett made a sharp turn off the roadway, onto a narrow dirt path.

Her heart hammered in her chest. "What are you doing?"

"Taking cover. We'll hide out in the thick underbrush."

It's Mason. She didn't give voice to her suspicion. Everett had heard her before and had ignored her. She doubted anything would convince him of the truth.

Braking to a stop behind a thick stand of trees, he killed the engine, opened the driver's door and held up his hand. "Stay here. I won't be long."

"But—"

"I want to see the car as it passes by."

He disappeared into the woods. Seconds ticked by as she waited and listened. In her mind's eye, she envisioned him approaching the highway and hunkering down in the underbrush.

Brakes squealed.

She startled. Her heart pounded even faster.

Placing her hand protectively on the baby's arm, she listened. Silence.

Had she imagined the sound?

The crack of a gun cut through the stillness.

Her pulse raced. A lump of fear filled her throat.

She saw Everett again in her mind, only this time he lay dead on the side of the road. Shaking her head, she tried to dispel the thought. Surely he hadn't been injured. Then a new realization hit. Mason—or whoever had fired the shot—would be able to find the SUV by following the tire tracks along the path through the forest. She and the baby would be easy marks and totally defenseless.

With trembling hands, she unbuckled the car seat and lifted Sofia into her arms. The baby sighed and snuggled close. Tears burned Natalie's eyes as she thought of what could happen if Mason found them.

After opening the door, she stepped from the car, not knowing where to go or where to hide. Her ears roared, and her pulse throbbed. An inner voice told her to run, but the undergrowth was too thick. Sharp thorns scratched her arms. She clutched Sofia even closer so the twigs and branches didn't hurt the little one.

Leaves rustled behind her.

She increased her speed.

Footfalls sounded, too close.

Her toe caught on a root. She started to fall.

Hands grabbed her.

She tried to struggle free.

"I've got you. You don't have to be afraid."

He was too tall and muscular. Not Mason, but Everett.

She gasped with relief. "What happened? I heard tires screech and a gunshot."

"A utility van. Pete's Plumbing, according to the logo on the side panel."

"Then it…it wasn't Mason?"

"A deer ran in front of the van. The driver had to put the animal out of its misery."

"I…I thought—" She trembled even more thinking what could have happened.

"The driver never saw me. I stayed undercover and watched it all play out. He took off after moving the carcass to the side of the road."

Everett rubbed his hands over her arms and peered at Sofia. "Is the baby all right?"

She nodded.

"Why'd you leave the car?"

Staring into his eyes, she suddenly saw her own mistake. His face was drawn with concern, but there was nothing threatening in his gaze.

"What's wrong, Natalie? Are you all right?"

His hands on her arms were strong, but his grip wasn't forceful or menacing; rather, it offered support and understanding.

"I...I thought someone was after us."

He pulled her close and wrapped both her and Sofia in his embrace. "I told you before, and you've got to believe me," he whispered, his voice thick with emotion. "I won't let anyone hurt you or the baby."

Tears blurred her eyes. She wanted to believe him more than anything, and for this brief moment, she leaned into him, drawing comfort from his strength.

"I should have stayed in the car, but I was afraid."

"It's okay," he soothed.

She pulled back ever so slightly and stared into his eyes. What she saw made her breath hitch, and for half a heartbeat she wanted to remain in his embrace forever. Too quickly, he slipped his arm over her shoulder and turned her back to the path.

"Let's head to the car. I want to get on the interstate and drive to Atlanta before traffic picks up. We'll grab some chow once we get there. You've got to be hungry."

She didn't answer him. She couldn't. She was trying to make sense of the confusion that swirled within her. Natalie wanted to believe Everett Kohl would help her, and hopefully, he was who he seemed to be. Having someone on her side would be a welcome change.

With his arm around her, they returned to the car. She settled Sofia into her seat and nodded her thanks when Everett closed the passenger door and climbed behind the wheel.

Leaving the underbrush, they gained access to the road again and, fifteen minutes later, entered the highway heading north to Atlanta.

Natalie's focus was on returning Sofia to her mother. She didn't know what would happen after that. She had to figure out her next step and whether it would include Everett. Was he working with her or against her?

EIGHT

Traffic was light as they drove along the interstate, which gave Everett time to review everything that had happened. He kept thinking about holding Natalie in his arms, which didn't help his focus. He still needed to make sense of the conflicting information. Mason was a CID agent who had done well for himself and risen in the ranks until he was in charge of an entire department in Vilseck. His subordinates had relied on him for sound leadership.

The military was a close-knit community. Surely if he'd done something wrong, the information would have followed him to Fort Rickman. Yet Frank and Everett had heard nothing that gave them pause.

Until Natalie entered the picture.

He glanced at Natalie sitting in the backseat. Her eyes were closed, and her head rested against the back of the seat. The tenseness in her face had eased as she'd fallen asleep.

Attractive as Natalie was, he could too easily be swayed by her blue eyes and engaging smile. Although today her mouth seemed set in a perpetual frown as if she was haunted by what had happened. Trying to elude a killer came with a high price tag, one that didn't lend itself to self-assuredness.

Seeing the signs for the airport, he switched lanes and turned onto Camp Creek Parkway. Driving past the long-term parking lots, he crossed the outer belt, heading for the shopping mall on the far side of I-285.

The sign for a mom-and-pop diner beckoned a welcome.

"Where are we?" Natalie's voice was thick with sleep as her eyes blinked open.

"Just past the airport parking. I thought we needed food."

She stretched her arms and arched her back. Hair cascaded over her shoulders and begged to be touched.

He tightened his grip on the steering wheel and turned into the diner parking area.

"What about meeting Wanda?" Natalie asked.

He glanced at his watch. "We're ahead of schedule, with plenty of time to grab some chow."

The smell of eggs and bacon greeted them as they entered the diner. A waitress ushered them toward a booth. Everett took the baby carrier from Natalie and settled it into the booster chair before scooting it close to the table.

Sofia opened her eyes and cooed. Everett's heart soared. With her dancing eyes and cherub smile, the baby made him forget the danger for a moment.

He laughed as her legs churned the air, and her tiny hands reached for him.

"Your daughter's adorable."

He looked up to find the waitress waving at Sofia. Her name tag read Rachel.

She glanced at Natalie and smiled. "You're a lucky couple to have such a precious daughter."

Natalie never missed a beat. "The baby stole our hearts the first time we laid eyes on her."

Glancing at Everett, she added, "Isn't that right, hon?"

He nodded. "That's right, dear."

"Can I bring you folks some coffee?"

Everett checked the menu on the whiteboard.

"Along with two egg-and-bacon platters. Add biscuits and grits."

He turned to Natalie. "Sound good?"

"Perfect."

"I'll place the order and be back with your coffee." Rachel hurried to the kitchen, and, true to her word, she returned with two piping-hot mugs, followed by their breakfast order.

Sofia slept while they ate and then sucked hungrily at her bottle when Natalie fed her after the meal.

Once the three of them had their fill, Everett signaled for the check.

"More coffee?" Rachel returned to the table and raised the carafe over his mug.

He held up his hand. "Just the check."

"It's been covered." The waitress glanced over her shoulder. "That nice man sitting by the door—"

Everett followed her gaze to the empty booth.

"Why, he must have left." Rachel seemed confused when she turned back to them. "He… he said you looked like such a nice family that he wanted to pay for your breakfast."

"Did you get his name when he signed the credit card receipt?"

She shook her head. "He paid with cash."

Everett glanced out the window at the parking lot. A dark sedan drove from the lot and merged into the traffic. The kindly patron, perhaps? Nice of the man to buy their breakfast, but the generosity had a strange feel to it.

He turned back to Natalie. "Let's get going."

The look on her face made him realize he wasn't the only one questioning the stranger's outreach.

"Did you notice anyone sitting near the door?" Natalie asked once they were back in the car.

"The only people I saw were two older ladies by the window and a couple of teens at the counter."

"I've got a funny feeling about what happened."

He wouldn't express his own concern but, like Natalie, he wondered about the benevolent stranger.

Everett kept thinking of the dark sedan as he pulled away from the diner and headed toward the long-term parking lots located just off Camp Creek Parkway.

"Your mother is going to be so excited to see you," Natalie cooed to the baby.

Everett checked the traffic, looking for anything or anyone suspect. He circled a couple of blocks and, once satisfied they weren't being followed, he headed back to the main road. Turning into the lot, he took the ticket from the automatic teller and drove to the numbered space in the rear where Wanda said she had left her car.

He glanced at his watch. Twelve-thirty. They had at least fifteen minutes to spare. He backed into a parking space so the front of the SUV was facing the entrance of the lot.

Turning off the ignition, he thought back to last night. Was Natalie right in suspecting that the killer—or killers—had followed him? If so, Everett was losing his edge.

He studied the other cars parked around them. Danger could be lurking anywhere. He had to be cautious. He knew too well what could happen when a cop lowered his guard or shrugged off information as being happenstance.

God, help me never make another mistake, he silently prayed. *Keep me vigilant and focused so nothing happens to Natalie or the baby.*

Time passed too slowly. Natalie glanced at the clock on the console and inwardly worried. Wanda was almost an hour behind schedule.

Sofia had fallen asleep, and Everett had stared nonstop at the entrance access to the lot until she wondered if his eyes were ready to pop. Occasionally, he glanced at her in the rearview mirror, which caused her neck to tingle. She averted her gaze and said nothing, feeling the tension mount as the minutes ticked by.

At frequent intervals, he studied the forested area behind the lot and stared at the cars on either side of them. Did he think someone was lying in wait?

Again, she glanced at the clock, willing the minutes to change on the digital. Finally, she could remain silent no longer.

"I'll call Wanda. Something must have delayed her flight." The call failed to go through. "Her phone must be off. I can call the airlines to check on the plane's arrival time."

He glanced at her over his shoulder. "You've got the flight number?"

She nodded. "And the direct line to flight information. At least we'd know if the aircraft has landed."

"Go ahead. See what you can find out."

She retrieved the number in her contacts and hit Call. An automated operator walked her through a series of prompts that required saying the city of origin, destination and flight number.

"The plane landed on time," Natalie said as she disconnected. "An hour and a half ago."

A muscle on the side of Everett's neck twitched.

"Maybe she had trouble locating her luggage." Natalie gave voice to a possible reason for Wanda's delay. Anything could have happened, especially with a killer on the loose.

As worried as Natalie had been about the baby's safety, now she turned her concern to the baby's mother. What if Wanda had been the target instead of Tammy? The killer could have entered the wrong side of the duplex and killed the wrong woman. Realizing his mistake, he could be at the airport waiting for an opportunity to finish what he had originally planned to do.

Natalie dropped her head in her hands and sighed.

"You're thinking too much," Everett cautioned.

"Then you must be, too. What if the killer entered the wrong side of the duplex?"

"You could play what-if all day, Natalie. Let's trust she's late because of her luggage. Or maybe the parking shuttle was delayed."

"And maybe someone convinced her to get in their car. As worried as Wanda has been about Sofia, she might not have realized that she could be in danger, as well."

Everett shook his head. "You're jumping to the wrong conclusions."

"Are you sure?"

He hesitated and then reached for his phone. "I'll call Frank."

"He's at Fort Rickman. How can he help?"

"He'll contact the local police."

"Who will question why we're sitting in long-term parking."

Everett lowered his phone. "Let's wait ten more minutes."

Time seemed to stand still, which added to Natalie's concern. Frustrated and worried, she finally scooted forward in her seat and tapped Everett's shoulder. "Call Frank."

Before Everett could grab his cell, the airport shuttle turned into the lot. They watched the van drive along the entrance road and stop a few cars away.

Natalie let out a deep sigh when Wanda stepped to the pavement. The driver placed her luggage beside her car and nodded his thanks as he accepted a tip. As soon as he drove off, Natalie opened the car door and waved.

Relief washed over Wanda's face. "The plane circled the airport until we got clearance to land, then we sat on the tarmac waiting for a gate to open." She hurried to the SUV. "Where's my baby?"

Bending down, she peered into the backseat and touched Sofia's cheek. "I have been so worried about you, little one."

Everett got out of the car, introduced himself and extended his hand as he approached Wanda. "I'm sorry you had to cancel your training class, ma'am."

"I needed to see my child."

"That's understandable." He smiled at Natalie. "But Sofia was in good hands."

"I know she was." Wanda squeezed Natalie's arm. "Thank you for taking care of her."

Everett glanced around the lot. "I suggest you and Sofia hole up in a hotel in the city until the CID and local police have some idea of who harmed Mrs. Yates."

Wanda nodded. "I can stay at the cabin."

"Negative." Everett hesitated. "Someone shot a bullet through the picture window this morning."

"Oh, no!" Wanda's hand flew to her mouth.

"We left immediately, and, as best I can

tell, no one followed us." He stared at the mother before asking. "Is anyone out to do you harm, ma'am?"

Wanda glanced from one to the other. "You think someone wanted to kill me and killed Tammy instead?" She shook her head. "That's preposterous."

"Your husband is deployed. Does he have any enemies?"

"Terrance? Not that I know of. My husband is a good man, liked by all."

"Perhaps someone from his past?"

"We've known each other since high school. As I said, he's a good man."

"You're sure no one is carrying a grudge? Perhaps something that happened in Afghanistan?"

"I'll confirm that with him, but I'd be surprised if that were the case."

"What about Mason and Tammy Yates? How well do you know them?"

"They moved in about three weeks ago and seemed like nice neighbors. She was a bit more outgoing. He's cordial but somewhat reserved."

"Did you ever hear them fighting?"

Wanda shook her head. "Never."

"Did they have visitors? Family ever stop by?"

"Tammy mentioned staying with her sister-in-law in Decatur until their quarters were ready."

"Did you get the sister-in-law's name?"

"Annabelle. She's single, no children. I would presume her last name is Yates."

"Did Mason and Tammy appear to be happy?"

"I really couldn't tell. They both were nice enough, and on the surface, their marriage seemed good. But then—" She glanced at Natalie and back to Everett. "Some things are hard to see on the surface."

Everett appreciated Wanda's candor. "The CID might be able to provide a safe house for you and the baby, if you need a place to stay."

"I've got family near Macon. We'll stay with them."

"Contact me once you're settled," Everett said. "We may have more questions."

He pulled out a business card and handed it to her. "Call me if you think of anything or anyone that might be suspect. I have your cell phone number and will keep you apprised of our investigation."

Natalie hugged Wanda, overcome with relief that mother and child had been reunited. "I'm so glad you could come back to Georgia,

Wanda. I know you were worried about Sofia. I was worried about you, too, especially when you were delayed so long, and we didn't know what had happened."

Wanda looked confused. "I thought someone notified you."

Natalie shook her head. "Who would have done that?"

"The man from Fort Rickman who called me."

Everett stepped closer. "Did you get his name?"

"I'm afraid not. He was very cordial. He wanted to know that I was all right. I told him I would be when I had my baby back in my arms."

"You told him we were meeting you?" Natalie asked.

"Was that a mistake? He said he was from the CID."

"Did you mention the location of the long-term parking lot?"

Wanda nodded.

Everett glanced over his shoulder.

"Let's get the baby into your car, ma'am. You and Sofia need to be on your way."

Wanda cuddled the little one while Everett moved the baby seat to her car. Natalie placed

Sofia's diaper bag and totes in the rear. Again, she hugged Wanda and watched as she shook Everett's hand. A heaviness hung over her as Wanda and Sofia drove away.

Everett hurried Natalie back to his SUV.

"Who called Wanda?" Natalie asked once she buckled her seat belt.

"I'm hoping it was Frank, but—"

"But it could have been Mason," Natalie said.

"It's unlikely, yet we don't want to take any chances."

"You said we weren't followed," Natalie reminded him.

"We weren't, but Wanda told someone how to find us."

He started the engine and after paying for their brief stay, he pulled onto the Parkway. "We'll take 285 south."

"Which heads to Interstate 75 and eventually to Fort Rickman."

Everett sighed. "Then we'll take the outer belt north and pick up I-20 East into the city."

She glanced over her shoulder. "I keep thinking we're being followed."

"At least Sofia is with her mother."

The baby was safe, but Natalie couldn't shake the sadness of having to say goodbye. In such a short time, she'd grown attached to the sweet little one. Hopefully, after the investigation was over, she'd be able to see her again.

"She's a cute baby," Everett said.

Natalie turned to face him. "They'll be okay, won't they?"

"I'm sure of it."

Driving north on the outer belt, she again glanced back, searching for anyone who might be following them. Was someone out there waiting and watching? If so, they'd know soon enough.

Where to now?

Anywhere safe, except Fort Rickman.

Everett's brow furrowed and his gaze flicked from the road ahead to the rearview mirror.

"Do you see something?" Natalie turned, glancing at the traffic behind them.

He shook his head. "Not really."

"Not really, yet you look worried."

"A feeling, that's all."

"A feeling we're being followed?"

Everett let out a stiff breath. "Maybe. There's a car about five vehicles back. The driver reminds me of someone."

Again she turned. "Is it Mason?"

"Probably not, but I want to make sure. He's

been behind us since we got on 285." Everett glanced at a road sign. "I'll take the next exit. We'll see what happens."

The exit appeared on the right. Everett waited until the last second and then swerved onto the ramp that curved up to a four-lane road. The stoplight at the top of the off-ramp flashed yellow. Without hesitating, Everett turned left and accelerated.

A dark sedan followed them but was forced to stop as the light turned red.

Everett crossed over the highway and turned left onto another ramp that led back to I-285, only this time they were headed in the opposite direction.

Merging with the flow of traffic on the highway, he glanced back. "We'll know if we fooled him in the next few minutes. Chances are he'll continue straight."

Natalie kept her right hand on the dashboard and watched for a dark sedan. "Did you see the driver?"

He shook his head. "He might not have been following us after all."

"You're saying that to ease my concern."

He nodded. "You're right."

"Maybe you should phone Frank and find out who knew we were meeting Wanda."

"Let's put a little distance between us and that car before I make the call."

They drove some miles without seeing the dark sedan. Everett turned back onto Camp Creek Parkway and headed to I-75, then turned north toward the city.

The Atlanta downtown area came into view. Tall skyscrapers stood out against the gray sky. The State Capitol appeared in the distance, the gold dome reflecting in the subdued afternoon sunlight.

Everett flicked his gaze to the rearview mirror to check that they had eluded the tail.

Could it have been Mason?

He glanced at Natalie. "Do a White Pages search on your phone. See if you can find Annabelle Yates's address. She might provide information about Mason and Tammy."

Natalie was successful, and a map search provided directions to the sister's home in Decatur.

"Will she talk to us?" Natalie asked.

"Depends on her relationship with her brother. Let's be careful what we reveal."

Natalie nodded. "Maybe you should do the talking. I'm liable to reveal too much, especially the way I feel about Mason right now."

Everett nodded. "Then follow my lead."

NINE

"Turn right at the traffic light." Natalie checked the GPS on her phone. "Eventually we'll pass Agnes Scott College on our right, and then we'll turn left at one of the next intersections."

"You've been here before?"

"Last Labor Day. I drove up for the Decatur Book Festival. Big-name authors gave talks, and booths were set up where vendors and publishers and local writers sold books."

"Do you read a lot?"

"When I have time. The festival had a number of children's authors, which is what interested me."

"You plan to teach high school?"

"Probably kids in middle school. They're just coming into their own, trying to be independent, yet totally focused on what their peers are doing. It's a tough time. At least it was for me."

"I was still fairly naive at that point." Everett smiled. "I didn't notice girls until I got to ninth grade."

"I bet all the young ladies had their eyes on you."

"Hardly. I was tall and skinny. The word *gawky* fit me to a T. Plus, I was totally clueless about the opposite sex, except that my sister was two years older and never wanted me to interfere with her life."

"You're close now?" she asked.

He smiled. "Very, and she lets me dote on her children."

"Proud uncle."

He nodded. "What about you? Any siblings?"

She shook her head. "Only child." She held up her hand and rolled her eyes. "No comments about being spoiled."

He smirked playfully. "Were you?"

"Spoiled?" She shook her head and picked at her jeans. "Hardly. There wasn't enough of anything to be spoiled about. My parents had little and wanted to be anything except a mom and dad."

"Hard for a kid, huh?"

"I pretended not to be bothered and developed a tough skin."

"Which you've shed."

"No one in the military cares about the past. We're all focused on getting the job done. That was a refreshing change for me."

"Do you ever go home?"

"No reason. My dad died when I was in Germany. He loved the bottle, but it didn't love him."

"And mom?"

"She called me a disappointment."

"You think she was sincere?"

"No reason to think otherwise. Some people shouldn't have children."

"Is that why you went into education? To help kids who might get shoved aside by parents who don't care enough?"

"That probably plays into it. I wanted to advocate for kids. Tell them they can succeed. To set their goals high. I wanted them to know their dreams can come true."

He kept his gaze on the road and was silent for a long moment. Natalie turned to look at the stores they were passing, knowing she'd shared too much.

What was it about Everett that made her feel

free to talk about her past? The entire time she'd been in the military, she'd kept her youth buried. No need to reveal the dysfunction that had been her life. She'd joined the military to get away and make something more of herself.

She'd almost succeeded, until Mason Yates stepped back into her life.

"I shouldn't talk so much," she admitted.

"I came from a good home and loving parents, but I was lucky. I'm sorry things were rough for you."

"I don't want your pity."

"Why would I pity you? You've succeeded to change your life. That's admirable."

"Unless it's for naught."

"Why do you say that?"

"Because I'm a person of interest in two murder cases. If Mason Yates has his way, I could end up in jail."

She'd said it, her darkest fear. She'd come close to being arrested in her youth and had strived to work hard in the military. Maybe she hadn't worked hard enough.

"We're not far." She pointed to the upcoming street. "Take a left at the corner."

Decatur was a pretty town with brick buildings and tall trees. They passed a park where people ambled along the sidewalk, pushing baby strollers while toddlers frolicked at their sides.

"Once the investigation is over, you can return to your classes and complete your degree. Student teaching comes next?"

"I've got two exams to take first, then the student teaching. I hope to apply for jobs next spring."

But everything had changed now that Mason had returned to Georgia.

"There." She pointed. "On the left."

A row of condos. The number on the side of the building matched Annabelle's address. "Her condo is second from the end."

Everett circled the block and pulled to a stop in an alleyway behind a row of homes. "We'll be less exposed if we use the back door."

Natalie glanced out the window. "She might not be home."

"Only one way to find out." Everett opened the door and stepped to the pavement. Natalie did the same. The air was fresh with a brisk breeze that caught her hair.

She pulled the wayward strands into submission and walked next to him along the sidewalk. He turned to glance around them, his right hand reaching under his jacket.

"Remember to follow my lead," he cautioned.

"You're in charge."

Natalie held her breath as Everett knocked three times. When no one answered, she felt a sense of letdown, discouraged that their trip had been for naught. She had started to turn away when footsteps sounded from inside.

Everett touched her arm with his left hand. She nodded and gathered her courage, not knowing what they'd find or who they'd see when the door opened.

"Ms. Yates?"

"Yes." The woman was tall and big boned, with long brown hair, streaked with gray, pulled back into a braid. Thick glasses perched on a too-sharp nose, and her thin lips were pulled into a frown.

Everett held up his identification. "Special Agent Kohl, ma'am. I'm with the Criminal Investigation Division at Fort Rickman."

Her shoulders drooped and grief flashed from her eyes. "You came because of Tammy."

"We'd like to ask you some questions."

"Didn't you talk to Mason? He's right there

on post. Surely you can find out anything you need to know by questioning him."

"He is being questioned, ma'am, but we wanted to talk to you, as well." Everett hesitated for half a second, before adding. "May we come in?"

She pushed open the screen door. "Of course, please overlook my lack of hospitality."

Everett stepped inside first and glanced around the airy and comfortable dwelling. The place was neat and clean and filled with a number of antiques. Turning back at Natalie, he held the door for her and nodded his approval, letting her know the house appeared safe. She stepped inside and stood next to him.

The sister pointed to the sofa in the living room. "Please, sit down. I could make iced tea or coffee."

"No need. We won't be long."

Natalie settled next to him on the couch, and Annabelle pulled up a side chair.

"Have you heard from your brother, ma'am?" Everett asked once they were seated.

"He called with news of Tammy's death." Annabelle shook her head, sorrow evident in her gaze. "I was worried about her, but I didn't think it would come to this."

"Ma'am?" Everett leaned in closer.

"She wouldn't listen to me."

Everett pulled a notebook and pencil from his pocket. "Mind if I take notes?"

"Of course not."

"Could you start at the beginning, ma'am?"

"The beginning was when Mason and Tammy met. Don't get me wrong, I liked Tammy, but she wasn't right for my brother."

"In what way?"

"She was an extrovert who needed people around her to make her happy. Mason is more subdued, introspective. He's always been a homebody. She was more a party girl who enjoyed socializing. I think she liked that aspect of military life, the social functions and get-togethers."

"Did you question the attraction when they were dating?"

"I did, but Mason was sure she was the one."

"You didn't agree?"

"I thought they didn't have enough in common."

"Yet they've remained married. How many years has it been?"

Annabelle thought for a moment. "Seven years. They were older when they met. Mason had been married before, and—"

Everett glanced at Natalie.

The sister noticed. "Is that a problem?"

"Could you tell me about the first wife, ma'am?"

"Janet Owens. I don't know her new last name. She remarried and moved to Pennsylvania."

"Were there children?"

"Mason said Janet didn't want to spoil her figure. She was pretty and petite and, according to him, quite self-serving."

"But she remarried?"

"That's what Mason told me a year or so after their divorce was final. Evidently he knew the guy. They had been stationed together at Fort Bliss."

"He was in the army?"

"A civilian. He worked with the Post Exchange there and then transferred to Pennsylvania. Mason mentioned an army college there."

"The Army War College in Carlisle Barracks, Pennsylvania?"

Annabelle tilted her head. "That sounds right."

"Do you know why your brother and Janet divorced?"

"Oh, no. I don't pry, and Mason doesn't discuss his personal affairs with me."

Natalie scooted forward on the couch. "It must have been a shock when you learned about Tammy's death."

"I couldn't believe how it had happened." Annabelle shook her head with regret. "They had stayed with me for a few weeks when they came back from Germany. Mason signed in at Fort Rickman, but the quarters weren't ready so Tammy remained here."

"How'd she seem?" Natalie asked.

"I don't want to say anything now that she's gone. Tammy and I were friends. She had a big heart."

"But what?" Natalie pressed.

"I sensed something was wrong. Then Vernon Ingalls stopped by."

Everett made note of the name. "Someone Tammy knew?"

"She grew up in Savannah and had dated Vernon before she met Mason. A few years ago, Vernon moved to Decatur. Somehow he learned Tammy was back in town and staying with me. I had been at the grocery and came home to find them having coffee. They both looked embarrassed, and I sensed something was going on."

"Like what?" Everett held the pencil over the notebook.

"Like a rekindling of their former attraction, perhaps."

"Did she see him again?"

"A number of times. I never asked, but I had the feeling she was trying to decide whether to stay with Mason."

"But she moved to Fort Rickman."

"That's right. Still, I worried about my brother being hurt again."

"What do you mean?" Everett asked.

"Our mother left us when we were young. Mason never got over the pain of being abandoned. Then when his first marriage didn't work, I wanted him to find happiness. Evidently Tammy got restless."

"Did you tell Mason that Tammy had seen her old boyfriend?"

Annabelle shook her head. "I kept that to myself. As you know, Mason has an important job and a lot of responsibility. He didn't need to worry about his marriage when he's under so much stress with his new assignment."

"It sounds as if you and your brother have remained close," Natalie said.

"He's all I have."

"How can we find Mr. Ingalls?" Everett asked. "I'd like to talk to him."

"He lives a few miles from here." She provided the address, then hesitated for a long moment. "Mason said the funeral will be delayed."

Everett nodded. "An autopsy needs to be done first. That could take time."

"Do you know where she'll be buried?" Natalie asked.

"There's a cemetery on the outskirts of town. We have a family plot. I presume Mason will inter her there."

"Does Tammy have family in the area?"

Annabelle shook her head. "She doesn't have anyone."

"What about Mason's first wife?" Everett asked.

"Janet's brother runs a restaurant in the heart of Decatur. The Peach Grill. You can ask for Danny, if you want more information."

Natalie and Everett stood and shook Annabelle's hand. "Thank you for talking to us today."

"What shall I tell Mason if he calls?"

The question took Everett by surprise. "Tell him the truth."

Her face darkened. "He won't like that I talked about him to strangers. Maybe I won't mention your visit."

Did Mason hold some type of control over his sister? "Whatever you think is best."

Leaving the house, Everett glanced back. Annabelle watched from the window as they hurried to his SUV.

She had provided the motive Everett needed to make his case against the special agent. If Mason learned Tammy was seeing Vernon Ingalls, he could have gone into a fit of rage and shoved Tammy down the stairs.

Natalie was right. Mason could have murdered his wife.

Natalie shivered involuntarily thinking of Tammy and how she had been pushed to her death.

"Are you cold?" Everett asked.

She shook her head. "I shivered because of what we learned. My heart breaks for Tammy. She screamed for help, but I didn't react fast enough."

"You ran next door and banged on the door. Then you called the military police. We're the ones who didn't arrive in time."

"Did you know Mason may have been involved when you got the call that night?"

"We knew there had been an argument at his quarters."

"So you were thinking about how to protect one of your own."

"Frank and I had our eyes open. We weren't hoodwinked by Mason or because he was a CID special agent."

"You heard what his sister said, Everett. Tammy was running around on him. I told you about his behavior toward me in Germany. If he thought his wife was unfaithful, no telling what he would do. Even push her down a flight of steps. Seems to me you have a reason to consider him a very likely suspect in his wife's death."

"After we talk to Vernon Ingalls, I'll call Frank."

Natalie let out a deep breath. In a roundabout way, Everett had admitted she was right, yet she didn't feel relieved or elated. She kept thinking about Tammy lying at the foot of the stairway. Instead of jubilation, she was overcome with sorrow.

TEN

As they wound their way through Decatur, Everett glanced at one of the side streets and spied the Peach Grill. "Annabelle mentioned Danny Owens's restaurant. Let's talk to her brother before we visit Mr. Ingalls."

They parked in front of the restaurant and hurried inside. The place was eclectic, a mix of country casual and upscale yuppie with stainless steel tables and chairs and rustic hand-painted signs on the walls.

A server greeted them. "Would you like a booth or a table?"

"We're here to talk to Danny Owens. Can you get him for us?"

"Your name?"

Everett held up his identification. "Criminal Investigation Division, Fort Rickman, Georgia."

The woman hustled into the kitchen and

returned with a tall man, early forties, on her heels.

He held out his hand and introduced himself then motioned them to a booth in the far corner, away from the few customers that were seated closer to the door.

"Is there a problem with one of my staff?" he asked as they sat.

"That's not why we're here," Everett said. "We're trying to locate your sister, Janet."

Surprise registered on his face. "Is she hurt? Is something wrong?"

"We need to talk to her."

"Janet doesn't live in Decatur."

Everett nodded. "I understand she moved to Pennsylvania. Could you give us her current contact information?"

"Mind telling me what this is about?"

"She was married to Mason Yates."

Danny nodded. "That's correct. He was a louse. I told her it was a mistake, but she refused to listen to what I had to say."

Danny hadn't let go of his anger. "When was the last time you saw your sister?"

"Janet hasn't been home since her divorce was final, and I don't blame her. Mason was caustic then. I doubt age has improved his outlook."

"You seem to harbor a lot of animosity toward your former brother-in-law."

"He was despicable. I wouldn't cross the street to see him."

"So you haven't seen him in how long?"

Danny's chest deflated. "Actually I saw him about a month ago. He came in here for a sandwich and beer."

"Did you talk to him?"

"I made it a point not to talk to him."

"Have you left town in the last twenty-four hours, Mr. Owens?"

His eyes widened.

"Just answered the question, sir. Where have you been in the last two days?"

"Working here in my restaurant. I stay late and arrive early in the morning. Why? Did something happen to Mason? If so, he deserved what he got."

"It wasn't Mason. It was his wife. She died yesterday."

The brother shook his head, visibly saddened by the news. "I knew Tammy. She was a good woman."

"How well did you know her?"

"She moved here after college and taught in the local school system. The teachers used to come to the Grill on Friday nights. That's how we met."

"Did you date?"

He shrugged. "We went out a few times."

"How many is a few?"

"Okay." He wiped his hand over the table-top and then glanced up. "We dated seriously for five months."

"What ended the relationship?" Everett asked.

"Mason. He came home on leave and stayed with his sister. Somehow he and Tammy connected, and as the saying goes, the rest is history."

"So Tammy broke off a relationship with you and started seeing Mason."

"That's right."

"Did Tammy know your sister had divorced Mason?"

Danny nodded. "That didn't seem to bother her."

"It must have been hard to take when Tammy dumped you for him."

Danny steeled his jaw. "I got over it."

Noticing he didn't wear a wedding band, Everett asked, "Have you ever been married?"

When Danny shook his head, Everett glanced quickly at Natalie and then back at the brother. "How did your sister hook up with Mason?"

"She went to Georgia State and lived in Atlanta. Mason was stationed at Fort McPherson."

"Which closed a few years ago," Natalie added.

"Exactly. They met at a bar. Janet liked the idea of a military guy. He was older and promised her the world."

"Are you still carrying a grudge against Mason for stealing Tammy?" Everett pressed.

Danny bristled. "Of course not."

"Especially since he had divorced your sister."

"Janet has moved on with her life. So have I."

"Where's your sister live now?"

"In Dahlonega. She remarried. Her husband works at the university in town. They have a couple kids. She doesn't need to reopen her past."

"We just want to ask her some questions."

He pulled in a deep breath. "And I don't want her hurt."

Everett leaned across the table. "Tell us how to contact her, or we'll bring in the local authorities and see if pressure can be put to bear."

"That's intimidation."

"Sir, women have died. We're gathering evidence. Talking to your sister might provide a clue into who's involved."

"It's Mason, isn't it? You think he's involved."

"Why do you say that?"

The guy shrugged. "I always thought there was something strange about him. Janet was young and naive. I was her big brother trying to keep her from getting hurt. I didn't do enough."

"You can't change a person's mind when they're determined," Natalie offered.

"Janet thought she loved him, but I knew that was a mistake."

Everett sighed. "We just want to talk to her, sir."

Danny nodded, and his shoulders sagged. He wrote her address on his business card and shoved it across the table. "I hope I won't regret this."

Everett read the address. "Her married name is Queen?"

"That's right. Her husband's name is Neal. They moved back to Georgia from Pennsylvania."

"Thank you, Mr. Owens. You can be sure justice will be served."

"Just so Janet isn't hurt."

"By the way," Everett added. "Did you see Tammy when she was staying with her sister-in-law a few weeks ago?"

"Only once. She stopped in the Grill with a local lawyer."

"Do you have a name?"

"Vernon Ingalls."

"How'd they seem?"

"Very cozy."

Everett pulled out his business card and handed it to Danny. "You think of anything I might need to know about Mason Yates or Tammy, call me. And don't leave town. I may need to talk to you again."

"Look, I didn't have anything to do with Mason for years."

"You served him lunch a month ago."

He nodded. "That's right."

"Then you've had contact with him. I'll be in touch."

They left and hurried to the car. A case was being built that painted Mason in a very bad light. Vernon Ingalls was a lawyer. Was Tammy seeing him because of a rekindled interested in an old boyfriend or because she planned to divorce Mason?

Surely Mr. Ingalls would have the answers they needed. At least, that was Everett's hope.

Pulling to a stoplight, Everett's cell rang. Natalie held her breath as he raised the phone to his ear after checking the screen. His face revealed nothing. Either he didn't know the caller, or he was trying to hold his emotions in check. "Special Agent Kohl."

He paused. "Thanks for getting back to me."

The light changed and Everett stepped on the accelerator. "You told them the CID in the US wanted the case reopened?"

The call must involve the *polizei* in Germany.

"Thanks, Tyler. Let me know when you hear anything."

He disconnected and glanced at her. "That was Tyler Zimmerman in Vilseck. The German police will review their files and will share any information they have with our folks on post."

"Did you learn anything new?"

"Not yet. Everything is going through the first stages of agreeing to work together. Tyler assures me he should have some information within the next day or two."

Would that be soon enough? "You didn't tell him what we learned about Mason."

"No reason to share that information with anyone in Germany until everything's been substantiated. That will take time."

She sighed with aggravation. "Everything takes time, doesn't it? Yet Mason's on the loose"

Everett shrugged. "A lot of things are adding up against him, but we can't rush the process."

He touched her hand. Not expecting the contact, she startled.

"Sorry." His face was wrapped with concern. "You're upset."

"Actually, it's more like confused. I don't know where you stand in all this. I need someone in law enforcement to navigate the system and find out exactly what happened to the woman in Germany, as well as Tammy. Denise's death needs to be solved, but I keep thinking it doesn't relate to the other two women."

"Unless Mason was your roommate's mysterious boyfriend."

Natalie shook her head. "Denise was a smart girl. Mason picks women he can control in some way, either through a work relationship or because they're lonely. Denise had friends and a good family. I can't see her becoming interested in an older man. Especially an older married man, like Mason."

"How long had she been seeing the new guy? Mason's been on post for six weeks."

She thought back to when Denise had first started acting secretive. Eventually she mentioned seeing someone new, but Natalie had suspected as much by that time. "The timing sounds right, but I still can't see them together."

Checking the GPS on her phone, she pointed to the next intersection. "Turn at the light. Vernon Ingalls's house should be halfway down the block on the right."

The residence was a circa 1940s two-story brick with a front porch and side patio. The home appeared to have been upgraded recently with new windows and decorative shutters. Wicker furniture on the porch looked inviting.

Natalie waited until Everett had parked and came around the front of the SUV before she opened the door and stepped to the sidewalk.

Together they hurried up the stairs to the front porch. He glanced over his shoulder as if to check that they hadn't been followed.

"You worry me when you do that," Natalie said.

"I'm just being cautious."

"Cautious and careful, but that still makes me concerned."

"Don't be. We seem to be the only ones around." He tapped on the door.

"We could call him." She glanced at her phone. "Want me to find his number?"

Everett knocked again. "Let's check the back door first."

Together they circled the house. A navy blue, four-door sedan sat in the one-car garage behind the home. A light was on in the kitchen. Everett double-timed up the rear steps to the small stoop. He pulled open the screen and tapped on the door.

When no one responded, he looked through the window.

"See anything?" she asked.

"There's a glass of what looks like iced tea on the kitchen table, half-empty."

Again he knocked.

"Excuse me." Natalie motioned him aside.

"What are you doing?"

"As I understand the law, you can't enter a building without a warrant unless you're invited inside."

Everett raised his brow. "Or unless I suspect foul play."

"And do you?"

"I don't think iced tea provides enough reason."

"Then I'll rest my hand on the doorknob and see what happens."

She pulled the edge of her shirt over her hand to keep from leaving prints and turned the knob. The door swung open.

Glancing at Everett, she smiled. "Easy peasy."

"An open door is reason for law enforcement to get involved," he said with a nod of approval. "Especially if Mr. Ingalls fails to respond. Stay here while I take a look."

Cupping his hand around his mouth, he called out, "Mr. Ingalls, this is Everett Kohl, Criminal Investigation Division, Fort Rickman. I'm coming inside, sir, to determine that you're all right."

Walking across the kitchen, Everett unlatched the guard on his holster and then peered into the living area. "Mr. Ingalls?"

Even from where she stood on the back stoop, Natalie could see the high ceilings and exposed beams in the main part of the house. Although an older home, it appeared well cared for, with lots of upgrades and a rustic charm she found inviting. Vernon Ingalls was evidently a successful lawyer to afford even the few expensive furnishings she could see from the doorway.

She stepped inside to get a better look, crossed the kitchen and stood for a long moment admiring the lovely decor.

Everett's voice came from what appeared to be an office or den at the end of the hallway. He backed into the hallway, phone to his ear and raised his hand to acknowledge her before he disappeared again.

Curious to see what he'd found, she hurried along the hall and peered into the office, taking in the mahogany desk and plush side chairs, the large world globe standing near the palladium windows and the shelves of books, many leather-bound.

Stepping fully into the room, she looked up at the exposed rafters. Her heart stopped.

In the corner, a man hung from a beam, his swollen face contorted in death.

She screamed.

Everett turned, his face drawn. He lowered the phone and grabbed her, ushering her back to the hallway and then into the kitchen.

"I didn't want you to see him."

"It's Vernon Ingalls, isn't it?" Her heart pounded. "Mason found out Tammy was seeing another man so he killed his wife and her boyfriend."

"There's another answer."

Natalie shook her head. "How can you think anything else?"

"Mr. Ingalls left a typed suicide note. He said if he couldn't have Tammy, no one else would, either. He claimed to have pushed her to her death last night. Today, overcome with remorse, he decided to take his own life."

"I don't believe it."

"I called the police. They'll be here momentarily. They'll alert the medical examiner who will determine the cause of death."

Suicide or murder? Natalie knew the answer even if Everett refused to see the truth.

He raised his cell to his ear once again. "Sorry, Officer, what were you saying?" He paused. "That's correct. The victim appears to have taken his own life."

Tears burned Natalie's eyes. Everett seemed oblivious to what had happened. Why couldn't he see this as a vindictive attack from a crazed CID special agent who couldn't handle rejection?

Her heart ached that an innocent man had died and no one thought Mason was to blame. Needing to distance herself from the pain of another death, she ran from the house. All she could see was the man's swollen body dangling from the rafter. Three people had died in less than twenty-four hours. Another woman had died a year ago. Yet no one saw the connection.

Without checking for traffic, she ran headlong into the street. Everett's SUV was parked on the opposite side of the road. She wanted to hide there, away from the crime scene and the smell of death.

From out of nowhere, a dark sedan sped straight toward her.

"Natalie!" Behind her, Everett shouted a warning.

She glanced back, seeing his mouth open, his arms flailing as he ran across the front yard.

The squeal of tires and roar of an engine drove away any other thought. Slowly, her mind tried to process the impending crash.

"Natalie!"

She wanted to respond, but she couldn't.

In a flash, he was beside her, grabbing her and shoving her out of harm's way. She fell to the pavement, but out of the path of the car.

The sedan squealed past. The driver gunned the engine and sped away, never slowing to find out if she was okay.

Everett reached for her. "Are you hurt?"

She couldn't respond. Her heart pounded too abruptly in her chest and her pulse thumped like a jackhammer.

She'd seen the driver of the car.

For a split second.

She'd seen Mason.

ELEVEN

The police questioned Natalie repeatedly, but she stuck to her story. The driver had worn a stocking cap on his head, yet she'd recognized him. Mason was the driver who had tried to run her down.

After the ME examined the hanging victim, police lowered the body and placed it in a body bag. Tomorrow an autopsy would be done. Everett asked that the findings be sent to the CID office at Fort Rickman. The medical examiner assured him they would.

The victim was Vernon Ingalls, a Decatur lawyer.

Everett shared the information he had received from Mason's sister with the local police, and two patrolmen quickly left to question Annabelle. Others knocked on doors and talked to the neighbors, in case anyone had seen anything suspect.

Stepping onto the front porch, Everett called post and informed Frank about the incident, as well as the dark sedan that had followed them earlier and their meeting with Annabelle Yates and Danny Owens.

Frank listened attentively and then sighed. "Sounds like you're building a case against Mason, but it's all circumstantial. I need concrete evidence, Rett."

"Has he remained on post all this time?"

"As far as I know."

"You're not certain?"

"He had an appointment with the chaplain about his wife's funeral."

"Did he show up?"

"I didn't put a tail on Mason, if that's what you're asking."

"Maybe you should have. The car that followed us and the vehicle that almost struck Natalie were dark, midsize, four-door sedans. Mason drives a navy blue car, which could have been on our tail."

"I'll find out if he's still on post, but you need to bring Natalie back here."

"Not yet, Frank. I need more time."

"It has to do with that first sexual harassment case, doesn't it, Rett? That wasn't your fault. You were ordered to close the investigation."

"Just like you're ordering me back to post."

"Okay." Frank hesitated for a long moment. "I'll give you twenty-four more hours. Then I want Natalie Frazier at Fort Rickman. Is that understood?"

"Roger that."

"And remember, Rett, you were a rookie back then. Now you're an experienced investigator. That makes a huge difference."

Except that only put more pressure on Everett. He disconnected and stood for a long moment staring at the road where Natalie had almost been hit. The driver had seen her, Everett felt sure, yet he had failed to slow down and had even seemed to accelerate at the last moment.

If Everett hadn't run after Natalie—

A ball of bile burned his gut. The thought of what could have happened wrapped him in a blanket of remorse. Natalie had been hysterical when he'd helped her to the side of the road. The near collision had been too close, and she'd been too emotional to see things clearly. As opposed as she was to Mason, Everett didn't know that she hadn't hallucinated and thought she'd seen the man at the wheel who constantly occupied her thoughts.

The lead officer tapped Everett's shoulder.

"We don't have any more questions. You might want to take Ms. Frazier home. She's looks worn-out and about ready to collapse."

Home? Women on the run didn't have a home.

The female soldier from his past had said something about her life being turned inside out. Surely that's how Natalie felt. The other woman had died long ago. Her body had been found in a deep ravine in the training area on post.

Everett had been the first at the scene.

Closing his eyes, he could still see her mangled remains. The sergeant major—her former lover—had beaten her with a baseball bat and left her to be eaten by animals and plucked by vulture birds—all because Everett hadn't done his job.

"Sir, did you hear me?" The officer leaned in closer.

Everett nodded. "You said Ms. Frazier can leave now."

"That's right. I'll call in the results of the autopsy to Special Agent Gallagher at the CID Office. I'll also pass along anything we get on the hanging victim."

"What about the suicide note? Did you locate a computer and printer in the house?"

"He had a laptop here but no printer. We're checking his office, which might turn up something."

"Any idea if Mr. Ingalls was going through a hard time?"

"We won't know anything until we talk to his business associates and neighbors. Perhaps friends in the area. We'll need information on the Yates death as well. Stranger things have happened than a man killing the woman he loves because he can't have her and doesn't want anyone else to, either."

"Messed-up idea of love," Everett threw out.

"You got that right. My crime-scene crew will be here through the night processing everything. Maybe we'll be lucky and find trace evidence that might provide more answers."

"That's what I'm hoping." Everett extended his hand. "Thanks for working with the CID."

"God bless the USA, right?"

"Exactly." Both men stepped inside. Natalie sat huddled on the couch. Her face was pale and her eyes downturned.

Everett gave the officer his card. "My cell's always on. Anything I can do to help, just call."

"Will do. You've got my number?"

"Already programmed in my phone."

"You're heading back to Fort Rickman?"

Everett glanced at Natalie. "I'm not sure."

"Safe travel."

"Roger that."

Everett neared the couch. Natalie looked up, her eyes rimmed with sorrow.

"We can go now."

She nodded and slowly rose.

"Did they determine if Vernon Ingalls committed suicide?" she asked, her voice almost a whisper.

"Not yet. They'll notify me as soon as they have more information."

She stepped toward the door and glanced though the side window. "It's so dark outside. How long have we been in here?"

Too long, Everett thought, taking her arm. "You need some food."

"I'm not hungry."

"We'll pick up fast food."

"I don't want to go back to Fort Rickman"

It seemed to be her mantra. "I understand."

She turned and glared at him. "Do you, Everett? Do you really understand? I think you're like all the other guys in law enforcement. You've got your own agenda. In your opinion, Mason is law enforcement, which means he can do no wrong. You're nice enough to me, but you're on his side."

"I never said that."

"You didn't have to. It's evident. I heard you talking to the other police officer. No one is concerned about Mason."

"I called Frank."

"And what did Frank do after talking to you? Did he arrest Mason?"

"Natalie, there has to be enough evidence."

"I saw his face. He was behind the wheel and almost ran me down. If I were a hit-and-run victim, would you be a bit more interested in who was driving the car?"

"I am interested. It's being looked into."

She sighed, the heaviness of her frustration evident.

They left the house and crossed the street to Everett's SUV. She glanced down at where she had landed after he had shoved her to safety. Her hands were scraped where she'd fallen to the pavement.

He hated that she'd been hurt, but she was alive.

For that he was grateful.

Staring into the darkness, he wondered what would happen next. Someone was after her. Was it Mason, or Denise's boyfriend, or some other perpetrator that didn't even have a name at this point in the investigation? No matter who it was, Everett had to make sure the perp didn't succeed.

Natalie's life depended on Everett's ability as a CID special agent. He couldn't let down his guard. Not tonight. Not tomorrow. Not the day following. Not until the killer or killers had been arrested and were behind bars. Then he could breathe deeply again.

But only if he'd done his job and kept Natalie alive.

Natalie huddled next to the door on the far side of the car and rested her head on the side window, her eyes focused on little except the darkness.

She'd refused Everett's invitation to stop for food. The last thing she wanted was to put anything in her stomach. The nervous agitation she'd felt since hearing the argument in the adjoining duplex quarters had grown even more pronounced with the lawyer's death until she felt completely overcome with grief.

Overcome with fatigue, too. She needed to sleep, but every time she closed her eyes she saw Vernon Ingalls hanging from the rafter. As hard as she tried to focus on something else, she kept going back to his puffy, contorted face.

Death was grotesque. Tammy's expression of pure terror had been more than horrific. Seeing a second person with that same expression was almost her undoing.

"Where are we going?" she asked, needing to fill the car with something other than the drone of the engine. Hearing her own voice—even if it wasn't much more than a whisper—meant she was still able to function, and the visions flashing through her mind were merely that.

"The North Georgia mountains. We'll stop in Dahlonega first and talk to Janet Owens Queen and then head farther north to visit my uncle."

"I don't like heights."

"Not to worry. Uncle Harry has a house on the side of a hill, overlooking a lush valley. The elevation isn't too high, and the trees should be showing signs of their fall colors. It's a good place to relax."

As if she could. "Is he expecting you?"

"More or less."

"Meaning he knows you're going to visit, but he didn't think you'd bring a stray."

"A friend, Natalie, that's what you are."

She shook her head. Everett was trying to

make light of her situation. "A woman on the run is more like it."

Glancing over her shoulder, she sighed with relief at the darkness behind them. "Appears we're the only ones on the road tonight."

"I've seen a few folks heading north, but the traffic's thinned out."

She glanced at the clock on the console. "It's almost nine o'clock, and we've still got a long way to go. Does your uncle know you won't be there until late tonight?"

Everett smiled. Even in the half-light, she could see the lift of his lips and his raised brow. She was beginning to read his expressions. The current look revealed a lightness of heart that she wished she could imitate. Right now, she felt too weighted down with worry.

"Uncle Harry expected me yesterday. I called and explained that I had to work. He assured me he'd be happy to see me no matter when I arrived."

"But he thinks you'll be alone."

Everett flicked a glance at her before turning his gaze back to the road. "He'll like you, Natalie. He never had any kids. Always wanted a houseful. He turned eighty his last birthday and plans to move to an assisted-living center closer to the city. He's not happy about leaving his home, but he knows it's a wise decision. I promised to lend a hand with getting his house ready to put on the market."

"And I pulled you away from helping him."

"It wasn't you. It was Tammy Yates's death and the investigation. But there's still time to help. Plus, you'll cheer him up. He always was a softy for a pretty face."

She tilted her head, surprised by his comment. No one had ever called her pretty. "My mother said I looked like my father. He was a stern man who never smiled unless he was nursing a bottle."

"Was she jealous of you?"

"What?" Taken by surprise, she adjusted herself in the seat. Her mother wasn't unattractive, but she did nothing to enhance her looks. Perhaps it was living with a drunk. She'd given up on life long before Natalie was old enough to understand what a dysfunctional family meant.

"Why would my mother be jealous?"

"She had to know how beautiful you were. Mothers usually take joy in their children. Maybe your mother carried her own hurt and couldn't see beyond her pain."

"So she stayed in a broken marriage because she didn't have anyplace else to go?"

"Did she take that out on you?" Everett asked.

The question hit home. "I never seemed to do anything right. I…I always thought I was the one at fault."

Thinking back to her youth, she mulled over what Everett had said. Maybe her mother had been the one with the problem instead of Natalie.

"You must have grown up with a lot of love," she said, thinking of the comparison between their lives.

"Love and acceptance. For years, I thought everyone had the same type of childhood. Once I got to the military, I learned the truth. Many folks struggle with issues from their past. They're looking for love but in the wrong places."

"Like the song."

He nodded.

"Evidently from what Annabelle said, Mason can't take rejection due to that long-ago hurt of his mother leaving him." She thought for a moment. "Is that a motive to kill his wife?"

"Maybe, if she planned to leave him."

"Then what about Vernon Ingalls? I thought you believed the suicide note he left."

"The police didn't find a printer in his house."

"That doesn't mean he didn't have access to one. Surely there were printers at his law office."

Everett nodded. "But would he have typed the note earlier in the day and then come home and fixed a glass of iced tea before he took his life?"

Natalie shrugged. "I don't know."

"I don't, either. But sometimes when everything looks too perfect at a crime scene, I start to question the reasons why. Death is usually not nice and neat."

"Vernon didn't appear to have struggled."

"Which doesn't rule out foul play. The medical examiner will do a toxicology screen on both the victim and the tea."

"Then you think he was drugged?" she asked.

"Perhaps. A visitor, someone he knew, could have slipped something into his glass to knock him out."

"Like Mason?"

"I don't know." Everett tugged on his jaw. "I'm just thinking about what could have happened."

"Okay, then let's what-if," Natalie suggested.

Everett nodded. "All right. Here's one possibility. If Mason killed his wife, he could have made a phone call to his own cell from his wife's phone after killing her. He leaves his house and drives to the track in the training area. No one sees him, if he's lucky…and he is lucky. Then he drives home and plans to notify authorities himself when he finds her at the foot of the stairs."

"Only I heard everything and called the MPs," Natalie added. "He's smart, thinks on his feet and changes the scenario to make it seem that an assailant has broken in and killed his wife."

"But there's no breaking and entering," Everett added. "Which means if Mason didn't kill his wife, then Tammy opened the door and invited the killer inside."

"So she knew him." Natalie thought for a moment. "But that's if someone else committed the crime. Mason is the most likely suspect in my opinion."

Everett shrugged. "You could be right—"

"But you don't think I am?"

He stared at her again for longer than she would have liked. "I don't know who's guilty."

Natalie's heart sank. In spite of his comment about her being pretty, Everett still thought of her as a person of interest. The compliment was to throw her off course.

She turned toward the window. Resting her head on the back of the seat, she closed her eyes, too tired to play games of what-if. Three recent deaths. Three murderers, perhaps, or one man who had a reason to kill at least two of the victims. Denise Lang was still an unknown. If only the cases could be solved. Natalie was tired of being on the run. She wanted everything wrapped up so she could move on with her life.

What about Everett?

He'd move on with his, as well.

Where would that leave her?

Alone again.

TWELVE

The tension Everett had been feeling eased the farther they got from Atlanta. Heading north into the mountains was a good decision. He and Natalie would have an opportunity to relax for at least a short time without worrying about a killer on the loose.

Thinking she must be asleep, he reached for his phone.

She lifted her head and stared at him. "Need to make a call?"

He nodded. "I wanted Uncle Harry to know he could expect us."

"Make sure you mention the woman you picked up along the way."

Everett chuckled as he clicked the prompt for his uncle's landline. He glanced at his watch. Knowing Harry, he'd still be awake.

He answered on the third ring. "Everett, tell me you're coming to see your favorite uncle."

"That's exactly right, sir. How are you?"

"Can't complain. I was afraid you wouldn't get away from that new investigation."

"Actually I'm bringing some of my work with me."

"Oh?"

"A woman who was involved in the case. She was the victim's neighbor. I knew you wouldn't mind."

Uncle Harry chuckled. "Is this woman also a person of interest in another way?"

Everett smiled. "Meaning?"

"Meaning, you're not getting any younger. I was eighteen when I proposed to your Aunt Rose. She was the prettiest girl in high school, and I wanted to lay claim to her before one of the other guys moved in."

"How could she have eyes for anyone other than you, Uncle Harry?"

"That's right. 'Course it took her two more years before she said yes, but I was first in line. Best thing I ever did was to claim her for my wife."

"I don't think today's woman likes to be claimed, sir."

"Nonsense. Every woman wants a strong

man who will take care of her. Even that woman you're involved with now."

Everett steeled his jaw. "We're not involved."

"Then *interested*. Is that a better description of your relationship?"

Everett wouldn't even call it a relationship. Interested? He stole a quick glance at Natalie. She was staring out the window as if she couldn't hear his end of the conversation, which of course she could. Hopefully, she hadn't heard what his uncle had said.

"We'll arrive in a couple hours. Don't stay up. I know where you keep the spare key."

"I'll be up, but maybe dozing in my chair. Pound on the door, and I'll hear you. A friend brought over some casseroles so there's plenty to eat."

"Was that Bessie Beyer?" Everett had met the lady who often brought his uncle food.

"You remember Bessie, I'm sure. She's a lovely lady. Also a good cook. She baked oatmeal raisin cookies, which are my favorite. There's ice cream in the fridge, so help yourself. I doubt you had time to eat."

"You know me too well."

"That's because you're just like your father. He invited me to visit, and I may take him up on the invitation. Anything to delay moving into that senior-citizen complex."

"You'll enjoy having neighbors nearby. Plus, there will be plenty of activities to keep you busy."

"I've got enough to do here in my house. No reason to create jobs just so I stay busy."

"We'll talk in the morning. Now get some rest."

Everett disconnected and placed his cell on the console.

"I've got a hunch that Harry wants to remain put and not move to Atlanta," Natalie said.

"I don't blame him, but he's getting older and he's fairly isolated."

"No sweet older ladies who could check in on him? You mentioned Bessie. Is she his age?"

Everett smiled. "A few years younger, and very active. She made a casserole that we can enjoy when we get there."

"Maybe that's the main reason he doesn't want to leave. I take it his wife passed away?"

"Five years ago."

"I'm sorry."

"So am I. Aunt Rose was a wonderful lady."

"You mentioned that they never had children."

"Uncle Harry said the good Lord gave them

many things but not children to call their own. Rose was a teacher. She said the students were her babies."

Natalie nodded. "That's one of the reasons I want to get my teaching certificate."

"You're not planning on having your own family some day?"

She picked at her shirt. Her hesitation made him wonder if he had said the wrong thing.

"I haven't wiped out the idea of getting married and starting a family, but I know things don't always happen the way we want them to."

"So you're taking matters into your own hands, if the right man doesn't show up?"

"More or less." She smiled. "Seeing the way my parents argued, I never had hopes of a happily ever after for my life. Besides, I was too interested in escaping the dysfunction and trying to make a life for myself that didn't include abuse."

"Your dad hurt your mom?"

"The other way around. My mother nagged him to death. Almost literally. I'm sure one of the reasons he turned to the bottle was to ignore her rants."

"And you were caught in the middle."

"That's it exactly." Natalie stared at the road ahead. "If you don't grow up in a happy home, it's hard to trust your instincts about love and forgiveness."

"I know about the lack of trust."

She stared at him as if waiting for him to explain more, but he wasn't ready to tell her or anyone about the mistake he'd made. Seven years, yet it seemed like yesterday.

"You recognized your mother's faults, Natalie, and you want that loving home you didn't have growing up. That means you'll try harder than others who have good things handed to them. You'll make your marriage work, and you'll provide a loving, stable home for your family."

"Time will tell." She smiled ruefully. "That's an expression my mother used, although usually she paired it with how I would fail at life."

"Was your father your advocate?"

"My father lived in his own world. Unfortunately, he didn't have enough energy or money to allow me into that world. I'm sure he wanted to do more for me, but he refused to stand up to my mother."

"Is that why you became so determined to be what your father wasn't?"

"Do you think I'm determined?"

He nodded. "Determined to prove your innocence. Determined to keep Sofia safe.

Determined to make a better life for yourself. That's all good."

"I never thought of it as being a good thing. I just thought it was what I needed to do."

Everett glanced at the rearview mirror. Seeing flashing blue lights in the distance, he pulled to the side of the road.

"What's wrong?" Natalie glanced over her shoulder and gasped. "It's the police."

"They're probably after someone."

She turned to him. "Did you tell Frank how to find me?"

"Relax, Natalie, they're not after you."

The squad car sped past them. When the outside lane was clear, Everett pulled back onto the highway.

Glancing down, he saw Natalie's hand gripping the console. She was trembling.

He took her hand in his. "You don't need to worry. The cop probably got a call about a speeder farther north."

She nodded and let out a stiff breath.

Everett squeezed her hand. "I told you, I'll keep you safe."

She eased back into the seat and pulled her hand away from his.

Everett's heart sank. Natalie still didn't trust him. Her actions proved as much. He thought back to the female soldier so long ago. She'd told him how her sergeant major boyfriend had threatened her. She believed Everett would keep her safe.

Only the evidence didn't corroborate her story about the sergeant major, and Everett had been ordered to close the investigation. A heaviness settled over his shoulders.

If he hadn't obeyed his superior, the woman would still be alive today. Everett had already made one mistake. He wouldn't make another, whether Natalie believed him or not.

THIRTEEN

"Dahlonega isn't far," Everett said, seeing the mileage marker on the side of the road. "We'll stop there and then head farther north to my uncle's house."

Natalie glanced at the clock on the console. "It's late. I doubt Janet will agree to talk to us."

"Three women have died. If Mason is the killer, she could be in danger. That might make her more interested in sharing information."

Natalie's eyes widened ever so slightly. "So you're beginning to believe me?"

"I never stopped believing you. But as I told you, I work with facts, Natalie, not supposition. The more we uncover, the more apt I am to believe he's involved. I'm not sure if he killed his wife or if he had anything to do with Denise Lang's death, but two women in the US and another woman in Germany are dead. Two of them have leads to Mason. Denise may be just a terrible coincidence."

"Except you said there are no coincidences in law enforcement."

He stared into the night. "That's it exactly. So we need to find how Denise fits into the picture. Hopefully, the Freemont police and the CID will find that missing segment of this story."

"Everything makes sense if Mason was Denise's boyfriend."

Everett nodded. "But you didn't think she'd be interested in him?"

Natalie raked her hand through her hair. "As I've said before, too often, I don't know what to think."

"So let's play around with what-if. Did Mason come on to her so he could get to you?"

"You mean he sweet-talked Denise to keep tabs on me?"

Everett nodded. "That's a very real possibility."

But one Natalie didn't seem to accept. She turned to stare out the window as if lost in thought. Before long, he heard the rhythmic pull of air, signaling she was asleep. The miles passed, and he thought of all that had happened until his cell rang. Frank's name was on the ID screen.

"Late-night call. What's up?" He kept his voice low. "Did you locate Mason?"

"He's at the Lodge getting some much needed sleep, which is what I should be doing."

"The downside of being in charge. You need to wake him up and haul him in for questioning."

"He's not going anywhere."

"I think he's already done too much."

"We'll get him first thing in the morning. Right now I've got other problems."

Everett's neck tingled. "Concerning Vernon Ingalls's death?"

"Negative. Remember Denise Lang?"

"How could I forget? Did you find the boyfriend? Is it Mason?"

"The Freemont police are handling the investigation. As far as I know, the secretive boyfriend remains a mystery."

"Surely someone's seen him. Freemont's a small town. Doesn't everyone know everyone else?"

"You'd think, only Denise and her honey didn't stay in town. They must have had a secret rendezvous spot in a neighboring town."

"Did the police talk to the folks at the restaurant where she worked? She could have confided in one of them."

"Could have and did are two different things. No one seems to even know about the guy."

"You don't sound convinced that he exists."

"That's it, Everett. If no one has seen a mysterious boyfriend, if the family hadn't heard mention of a new man in her life, if she's never been spotted in town with some new guy, I start to wonder if he wasn't a figment of someone's imagination."

"Denise made him up? But why? So she could claim someone was attracted to her?"

"I don't think Denise is the one with the imagination."

"Meaning what?"

"Meaning the only person who has mentioned a boyfriend is Natalie. Perhaps it was convenient to have another person of interest in the case."

Anger washed over Everett. He was tired and frustrated with an investigation that wasn't going anywhere. He and Frank had worked together in the past, and he'd always thought of him as a friend, but the power of being in charge while Wilson was away was messing with his head. "That's the most ridiculous thing I've heard of in a long time."

"You're not seeing things through my eyes, Rett."

"I'm seeing things very clearly."

"You want to believe Natalie."

"Correction, Frank, I do believe her."

"She's pretty and somewhat needy."

Again, he bristled. Of all things, she wasn't needy. She was determined and forthright and her own woman. She didn't need him or anyone else for that matter. She relied on her own ability. "She's strong and self-assured, Frank, and also truthful."

"It's that first case you covered. You still blame yourself."

"I blame a superior officer who told me to end the investigation. As soldiers we're taught to comply with our commanders, which is what I did. The military code of justice never talks about the guilt when a soldier follows orders that aren't sound."

"The sergeant major seemed squeaky clean."

"Looks can be deceiving. Case in point, Mason Yates. He looks like a competent CID special agent, but he's got a history of corruption and poor judgments. If you talked to someone in the CID office in Germany, you'd know he isn't who he seems."

"Because of the woman who died?"

"Exactly."

"I have been in communication with our folks in Vilseck. They're getting the information from the *polizei*."

"Did they tell you that Mason came on to Natalie after the woman's death?"

Frank hesitated for a long moment.

"Evidently they didn't."

"They told me rumors had circulated."

"That's right."

"Only the rumors said Natalie was the aggressor in the relationship, and Mason was the one who tried to keep her at bay."

"That's preposterous."

"Open your eyes, Everett. See her for who she truly is."

"I am seeing clearly."

"There's something else you need to know."

The tone in Frank's voice made Everett's stomach tighten. He didn't want more unfounded remarks or rumors about Natalie. "What is it?"

"The Freemont police located video from the apartment complex where Denise and Natalie lived."

"Did the video show the killer?"

"I'm not sure." Frank hesitated.

"What's that mean?"

"A woman was seen hurrying to the apartment Dumpster the day Denise died."

"A woman?"

"That's right. She dumped a bag into the trash."

"She? Who is she?"

"The police dug through the garbage and found the dropped bag. It contained clothing."

Everett waited.

"Blood-covered clothing."

"You mean the clothes the killer may have worn?"

"It appears that way."

"So it was a woman? Did the police identify the person in the video?"

"The clothing was covered with blood that matched Denise's blood type and Rh. DNA testing is being done."

"Who was the killer?"

"The clothing belong to Natalie Frazier."

"What!" Everett wanted to pull the car to the side of the road and pound the steering wheel. Instead, he kept his eyes on the road and the SUV heading north.

"Who the clothes belong to doesn't have

anything to do with being a murderer. Besides, videos can be doctored."

"Everett, face the facts. It appears Natalie was involved in her roommate's death."

"Did you see the video?"

Frank blew out a stiff breath. "I did."

"Did you see Natalie's face?"

"I saw enough to know it was her."

"You didn't see her face. You saw someone who could have been Natalie but who wasn't."

"Everett, you're parsing words."

"I'm parsing the truth."

"She needs to come back to Fort Rickman."

"Have you hauled Mason in for questioning?"

"Not yet."

"Then I'm not bringing her back to Fort Rickman. Not until we have more information."

"You're not thinking straight. She's got you hoodwinked."

"That's crazy."

"We don't have evidence to tie her with Tammy Yates's death, but this video makes her more than a person of interest in her roommate's death. I want her back at Fort Rickman."

"Give me more time, Frank."

"She needs to be turning herself in on post or to the Freemont police."

"I'll take that into consideration."

"Everett, don't be foolish."

"I'll be in touch, Frank."

"Don't make a mistake and let her sway you to do something against good investigative training."

He disconnected and turned to find Natalie staring at him.

"What did Frank tell you?"

"We'll talk about it later. Go back to sleep."

"Sure?"

"Cross my heart."

She smiled. "My dad used to say that when I was a girl."

"A nice memory, right?"

She nodded and dropped her head back on the headrest.

Natalie couldn't have been involved in her roommate's death. Frank had to be wrong. Everett didn't believe the video.

Please, Lord, let Frank be wrong.

Natalie opened her eyes again when Everett turned off the highway. They wound their way along a narrow two-lane road that led to Dahlonega. The road edged a creek and wound up the mountain. In the distance, giant floodlights illuminated the golden spire of one of the university buildings, bringing a sense of welcome to the darkness. Passing the campus on the left, they headed into the small town and circled the square.

Natalie checked the GPS on her phone. "Turn right at the next corner."

Everett glanced at the few people on the street this late at night, and the city hall in the middle of the square. "Looks like a nice town."

She nodded. "The university has a great degree program in education. I thought about moving here at one time."

"But you decided to stay in Freemont?"

"Classes opened in the local area. Teaching jobs are a bit easier to come by in Freemont. I was thinking of my future." Although she'd probably made a bad decision. If she'd moved to Dahlonega and attended school there, she wouldn't be in the middle of a murder investigation.

"This used to be a gold-mining town," she said. "They still have areas where tourists can pan for gold."

"Sounds like fun."

"Kids love it the most."

Everett chuckled. "I'm sure."

"Turn right at the next intersection. The

house should be halfway down the block. Number 210."

Everett spotted the number on the mailbox and pulled to the curb.

Natalie stared for a long moment at the two-story house with a wide porch and potted flowers. Her heart lurched as she thought of the lovely setting and what she'd hoped her life would include someday. "Nice place. Looks like small-town Americana and happy home."

Everett eyed her. "Do I note a hint of envy in your voice?"

"Not envy, just admiration for someone who escaped Mason and, from all appearances, made something better of her life. I had hopes for my own, but it doesn't appear to be shaping up the way I wanted."

"It's not over yet, Natalie. Stay optimistic."

She nodded. "You're right. Maybe Janet will provide another piece in the puzzle so you'll start to believe me."

He grabbed her hand. "Haven't we been down that road before? I believe you. I just need evidence to establish Mason's guilt."

She let out a deep breath. "Okay. You're right. I'm tired and frustrated by all of this and wondering what Janet will provide."

Everett pulled the key from the ignition and

walked around the car to open the door for her. She liked the attention. In fact, there was so much about Everett that she did like, which wasn't a good thing. She'd steeled her heart for so long and convinced herself she didn't need a man to make her happy. She could be happy on her own. Except that wasn't working out for her.

At least not recently.

She shoved the thought aside and stepped to the pavement when he opened the door. A hint of aftershave wafted past her as she hurried to the sidewalk. She needed to distance herself from anything that played havoc with her emotions, which was what she felt at the moment. She blamed it on fatigue and a mix of fear and worry.

She didn't need anyone in her life, she told herself again. She didn't need Everett.

But when he put his hand on the small of her back and walked next to her up the stairs of Janet Queen's lovely front porch, Natalie couldn't escape the desire of needing more to life than she had.

She wanted a life filled with love and happiness. At this moment, she realized she wanted a good man—like Everett—to be part of that life.

FOURTEEN

Everett tapped on the front door and stood protectively in front of Natalie. A tall man with a beard and glasses, probably fortysomething, opened the door with a quizzical gaze.

Everett held up his identification. "Sir, I'm Everett Kohl, Criminal Investigation Division, Fort Rickman, Georgia. I'd like to talk to Janet Queen."

"Fort Rickman? You're a long way from home."

Everett nodded. "Yes, sir."

The guy glanced at his watch. "It's late. Would you mind explaining why you need to talk to my wife?"

"Sir, it involves an investigation. I'd like to ask her a few questions. I understand it's late, but we've traveled a long way."

"Neal?" A woman walked up behind the man. Black hair, blue eyes, small frame and moderate height. She reminded Everett of Natalie in her bearing.

"Janet Owens Queen?" Everett asked, holding up his ID again. He repeated the introduction he had given the husband and then introduced Natalie. "We're investigating a case and need to ask you a few questions."

Her brow knit. "I don't understand."

"Could we come in?"

She glanced at her husband and nodded. He pulled open the door and pointed them to a living area. "You can talk in there."

"Who is it, Mom?" A young teen with long black hair and eyes as large and as blue as Janet's peered down at them from the stairway. "What's going on?"

"It's okay, honey." Janet smiled confidently at her daughter. "Finish your homework. These folks just need to ask me a few questions."

The girl stared at them for a long moment and then shrugged. "Whatever."

Janet motioned them into a cozy living room with overstuffed furniture and soft lighting from two ceramic lamps. The tables on each side of the couch matched the coffee table and were crafted from a rich, dark wood. The rug was plush, and watercolor paintings of mountain scenes decorated the wall.

"Your art is beautiful," Natalie said as she admired the paintings.

Janet smile halfheartedly. "Thank you. I dabble at times."

"You're the artist?"

The woman nodded. "It's something I always wanted to do, but never had time until recently."

"You're very talented."

The woman's face softened, and she motioned them toward the couch, while she sat in an overstuffed chair identical to the one her husband had chosen.

"You mentioned traveling a long way," Janet said, once they were seated. "Would you care for a cup of coffee or hot tea?"

"We appreciate the offer, ma'am, but we're fine." Everett scooted closer to the edge of the couch and stared at Janet a long moment before he spoke.

"Your brother gave us your address, ma'am. He was guarded at first, but eventually realized we in no way wanted to upset you or bring harm to you or your family."

"What's this about?"

"Mason Yates." Everett glanced at her husband and then back at Janet.

She toyed with her wedding band. "Neal is

well aware of my first marriage, Special Agent Kohl. I don't have any secrets from him."

"Yes, ma'am."

"Is Mason in trouble with the law?"

"Why do you ask?"

She shrugged. "Stands to reason. You're involved with military law enforcement. Mason is, as well. I doubt you'd travel so far for information unless he was suspected of some wrongdoing."

"What kind of husband was Mason?" Everett glanced at Neal. "I understand that might be a difficult question."

"I was young when we met. Mason was older. I haven't seen him in years, but in his youth he was an attractive man. Tall and muscular. I attended two years of college and wanted to get on with my life. Mason swept me off my feet, as the saying goes. He was attentive and persuasive."

"Persuasive?" Everett asked.

"Perhaps I should say possessive. Looking back, I realize he isolated me from my family. My brother and I had been close. I'm ashamed to say that Mason convinced me to stop seeing Danny, claiming my brother didn't want me to be happy."

"Your brother was against the relationship?"

She nodded. "He thought Mason was domineering and manipulative."

"Was he?"

"Yes. Of course, it took me a while to realize the truth. We had one car that he took to work. If I wanted to go anyplace, even the grocery store, he made it sound like an inconvenience and unnecessary. He always drove me, which at the time I didn't realize was a way to control me. Mason can be engaging if it suits his needs. Before long I had no one else in my life. We had moved to Fort Huachuca, Arizona, so I was far from family. We lived off post in a small house away from any neighbors."

She glanced at Everett, her eyes heavy with remorse. "By the end of our first year, I was well aware of the mistake I had made. Getting away from him was another matter."

"Was he abusive?"

"Not physically."

"Verbally?"

"A bit. Conversation was limited to topics he wanted to talk about. Anything that would bring joy to our life together wasn't of interest to him. I began to think something was wrong with me, that I was to blame for the unhappy marriage."

"He was controlling," Neal inserted, his

face drawn with the reality of what Janet's life had been.

"You eventually divorced," Everett stated.

"Thankfully." She nodded. "Mason went TDY to Fort Lewis, Washington, for six weeks."

"He left you the car."

"No. He drove the car to the airport and left it there. He said I had enough food in the house to survive until he returned."

Everett glanced at Natalie. She was taking in everything Janet said.

"Did you contact family?" Everett asked.

"A woman who lived a few miles away helped me. She took me to her church and put me in contact with a lawyer. They called my parents, and my father wired money so I could fly home."

"What happened when Mason returned?"

"He came to my parents' house and insisted he needed to see me. My father had a shotgun. He told Mason he'd use it if he ever appeared in the area again."

"And did he stay away?"

She nodded. "Mason did, although his sister came to visit me. She tried to get me to go back to Mason. She said he was hurting and sorry for not being the husband I wanted. She said he promised to change."

"Did you have a good relationship with Annabelle previously?"

"I never thought she approved of me. Before we married, he and I joked about our siblings who were trying to stop the wedding. Later I realized Danny was looking out for my well-being."

"What about his parents?"

"Mason's mother died the year before we married. She had abandoned her children when Mason was a child. The father took care of them as best he could, but I think a lot of the household responsibilities fell to Annabelle."

"Did Mason talk about his mother?"

"Only that she had left him. He didn't show emotion the few times he mentioned her. I thought he should go to counseling, but he said he didn't need a shrink."

"Yet you saw the need for psychiatric help?"

"Only because he had been abandoned. I felt that played into his lack of trust. If he worked through the pain of having his mother leave him, I was convinced he would learn to accept other things, as well."

"Growing up, did Mason ever try to contact his mother?" Everett asked.

"Not that I know of. Evidently she hadn't moved that far away. When he was young, he kept imagining she'd come back."

"Have you seen Mason or his sister in the last few years?"

"Not since we divorced."

Everett pulled a business card from his coat pocket and handed it to Janet. "Call me if you think of anything else that might have bearing."

"You never told us why you wanted information about my marriage to Mason."

"I'm not sure if you're aware that Mason remarried. His second wife died recently. I'm investigating her death."

"Then it wasn't by natural causes?"

"That's what I'm trying to determine." He stood and shook her hand and then her husband's. "I'm sorry to disturb you this late at night. Thank you for your cooperation."

"If you don't mind me asking," Janet said as they neared the door. "How did she die?"

Everett glanced at the stairway leading upstairs where the young daughter stood staring down at them. "She fell."

He opened the front door and then turned for a moment to stare again at the steep stairway.

"Tammy Yates fell down the stairs to her death."

Janet gasped, her hand clutched her husband's.

"Thank you for seeing us." Everett nodded in farewell. "Be sure to call if anything else comes to mind."

He and Natalie stepped onto the porch. Before he could close the door behind them, Janet grabbed his arm. Turning, he saw fear in her eyes.

"I told you Mason's mother died a year before we were married."

Everett nodded. Noting Janet's concern, his gut tightened. "How'd she die?"

"She fell down the stairs to her death."

Everett and Natalie hurried to his car. Had Mason killed his mother? If he was as manipulative as Janet claimed, his dysfunction had surely escalated with time.

Luckily Janet had freed herself from his hold.

He glanced at Natalie. Hopefully, she would be able to do the same.

Leaving Dahlonega along the winding, narrow road, Natalie couldn't talk. She kept thinking of Janet and what she had experienced with Mason.

Everett skirted the main highway and took another back road and then another so that she had no idea if they were headed north or south. Just so they weren't headed to Fort Rickman.

Everett seemed equally lost in thought.

A full twenty minutes after leaving Janet's house, he turned to her. "I believe you, Natalie."

She nodded. That statement had been long in coming, but Everett needed facts and evidence before he would buy into something, even something that might seem perfectly clear to others.

"He's dangerous." Everett sighed.

"Tell that to Tammy Yates and Paula Conway in Germany."

"Tammy was involved with Vernon Ingalls. If Mason found out about him or if Tammy was forthright with the information, he could have exploded."

Natalie nodded. "I told you they argued."

"You said the voice was deep and insistent, but you weren't sure it was male."

"I was sure it was antagonistic. Whether I recognized the voice or not, it was Mason railing at Tammy."

"I need to tell Frank."

"Will he believe you?"

"Why wouldn't he?"

"You've told him other things about Mason, and he hasn't reacted."

"Janet corroborated information about Mason being suspect."

He picked up his phone, checked the coverage and then shook his head. "Looks like we're too far from a cell tower."

Natalie looked at her phone. No coverage, either. "Seems strange to find areas where cells don't work. We've become so used to them."

"The mountains and the weather cause reception to be spotty. We'll be at my uncle's house before long. If the cell connection isn't strong enough there, I'll use his landline."

What would happen when Everett passed on the information to Frank Gallagher? Would he be able to convince the other CID agent about Mason being a person of interest?

Everyone had been so quick to point a finger at Natalie. Now, they needed to turn that finger to Mason. He was the suspect in his wife's murder and in the woman's death in Germany. Denise's murderer was still at large.

Could Mason have killed three women and his mother? She shivered, realizing he had tried to kill her, too. Until he was behind bars, she'd have to live looking over her shoulder. That's not what she wanted.

She wanted a home filled with love and joy. She wanted a man to stand by her side and help her through the ups and downs of life. She wanted to put her faith in a guy she could trust.

What about her faith in God?

She needed that, as well.

Staring into the darkness, she lifted her gaze to the starry sky. *Wherever You are, Lord, I hope You can hear me. I've tried to find my way in life without turning to You, which hasn't worked out for the best. I need someone on my side. I'm beginning to realize I need You, Lord.*

FIFTEEN

Everett left the main highway and turned onto a narrow two-lane road that led up the mountain. Natalie glanced out the side window. The moon poked through the cloud cover and showered light into the valley below.

Just as she had told Everett, she didn't like heights, and she didn't like driving up the side of the mountain that had a huge drop-off. She struggled to avert her gaze and quell her upset stomach.

"I thought you said your uncle lived on a gently sloping hill?"

"He does, but we need to climb to a higher elevation before the incline tapers off."

"You're trying to scare me."

Smiling, he reached for her hand. His touch warmed a place deep inside her that had been cold for too long.

She didn't know if Everett was telling her

the truth or playing her for a fool, but the small gesture that seemed so inconsequential did something to her internal compass. Right now it was swirling around without knowing where to stop.

Being with Everett was unsettling. His understanding and warm gaze had her confused and not knowing where she was headed.

He'd said to trust him, which she wanted to do, but after everything that had happened, she couldn't trust anyone.

Even a CID agent who told her she was pretty and brought a moment of light into the darkness of her life.

Would he turn on her and take everything she had said and twist it into evidence that would send her life spiraling out of control? Everything inside her shouted a resolute no, yet she needed to be careful.

Again she stole a glance out the window and cringed at the steep drop-off. Tammy Yates and the woman in Germany had both fallen to their deaths. Just so Natalie didn't lose her life falling down the side of a mountain.

She closed her eyes and rested her head on the back of the passenger seat, unwilling to glance at the deep gorge that even in the moonlight looked threatening.

"We're almost there," Everett eventually announced.

She opened one eye and nodded, seeing the house perched on a knoll in the distance. "I thought you said his home was in a clearing."

"It is, just don't look over the edge."

"I'm trying not to." Every time she glanced right, her stomach rolled. What would happen when she saw the drop-off in the light of day?

She turned to him, and he reached for her hand as if to give comfort.

"You said your uncle was eighty years old. How does he get up and down the steep incline at his age?"

"He's like a mountain goat." Everett chuckled. "It doesn't seem to bother him, and he keeps a heavy foot on the gas pedal."

"Remind me not to accept a ride with Uncle Harry."

She glanced again at the mountain home. Lights glowed from the downstairs windows and brought warmth to the chill of the night.

For so long, she'd yearned for a place to call home. Her father had died when she was in Germany. No telling what had happened to her mother.

She had a need to share with Everett what

she was thinking. "When I came back from Germany, I called home."

He nodded, although he kept his eyes on the road, which she appreciated. She didn't want his focus to be pulled away from the narrow path that edged the steep cliffs.

"The phone had been disconnected."

"Maybe your mom changed to a cell instead of a landline," Everett offered.

"Perhaps she didn't want me to find her."

"Is there anyone you can contact? Like an old neighbor who might have information about your mom?"

"I…I didn't try." She tugged at her hair. "I'm not sure I wanted to know what had happened to her. If she was in need, I would have to help."

"The Good Book tells us to honor our mother and father."

"I know. That could be why I didn't try to track her down. You're a good man to help your uncle."

Everett laughed. The sound filled the car and made her smile. "He's a great guy. I'm lucky to have him in my life."

"Your dad's brother, right?"

"Older brother. Dad's a young sixty-five.

There were three boys. The oldest brother died in Vietnam."

"I'm sorry."

"War happens."

She nodded. "Were you in Afghanistan?"

"And Iraq. How 'bout you?"

"One thirteen-month deployment, but I was lucky."

"God took care of you."

She stared at the strength of his jaw and his steady gaze. "Like He took care of you?"

Everett nodded. "Exactly. My parents are my biggest prayer warriors. At times, when things were tense, I could feel their prayers."

"In what way?"

He hesitated. "A sense of not being alone, as if I was surrounded by a shield of their love."

"That's hard for me to understand. I seem to always be looking over my shoulder, trying to push ahead, yet worried about what I've left behind."

"Unresolved issues, maybe?"

She thought back to the life she'd left. "I left Detroit without looking back. That was a good thing."

"Did you say goodbye to your mother?"

She shook her hand. "She was glad to get rid of me."

"You're sure?"

"I am, but it still stings when I think of what I didn't have growing up."

"Have you forgiven her?"

"What?"

"Forgiveness. It's therapeutic, healing. Maybe you're looking back because you haven't dealt with all the issues of that time."

She shook her head, then peeked down the dark side of the mountain. Her stomach roiled, and she turned away from the window. "It's resolved because it's over."

"Is it?"

"Yes, of course."

"But you brought it up," he said.

"I don't understand."

"You mentioned your mother and what you'd left behind because it's still bothering you. You can't close the door when you're holding it open."

"I slammed it shut when I walked away."

"No, you didn't, Natalie. Maybe it's only open a crack, but your foot's still on the threshold. You're not willing to close off the past. Not yet."

Frustrated, she wrapped her arms around her waist. "You don't know what you're talking about."

"Because I came from a happy home?"

"Maybe. Or maybe you don't see things clearly. You drive me all over Atlanta and then into the mountains. I don't get it. It's not that you think I'm innocent."

She expected him to correct her. When he didn't she felt even more unsettled. "Do you think I'm involved, so you're sticking close? It's easier to stay with me so you know where I am. Then when Frank snaps his fingers and tells you to bring me back to Fort Rickman, you'll turn south and do what he tells you."

Everett clenched his jaw.

Realizing she'd made a mistake being so vocal, she touched his arm. "I'm sorry. You've done so much for me. I shouldn't have said those things."

"You're tired and probably hungry even though you didn't want to get anything to eat in Atlanta."

"You're making excuses for me."

"I'm giving you the benefit of the doubt." He hesitated for a moment. "I'm concerned about your well-being, Natalie. If what you said about Mason coming on to you is true, I need to make sure the military tracks down the facts and the guilty are caught, namely Mason Yates."

"I remember meeting Mason's wife and thinking how pretty she was and what a nice couple they seemed to be. Appearances can be deceiving, as I know too well, but he seemed to have it all. At that time, he was well-thought-of in the CID. He had a lovely wife. A teacher who was a positive influence in a lot of children's lives. They lived off the *kaserne* in a nice area of German homes. I used to drive by his house and imagine how life would be if I could have just a portion of what he had, if I'd ever get my life on the right track. I thought of the happiness they shared and the love that must exist between them."

"You drove by his house?"

She nodded. "Silly, wasn't it? He lived in the next little village that I had to go through on my way to the military *kaserne*."

"Did he ever see you?"

"I doubt it. Why?"

"Maybe he read something more into your drive-by."

SIXTEEN

Once they arrived at his uncle's home, Everett opened Natalie's door and grabbed her tote from the rear of his SUV, then walked her up the steps to the wraparound porch. He glanced back. The moon peered between the clouds and exposed the expansive valley below. The pristine scene was breathtaking.

Inhaling the crisp mountain air, he sighed. "It's like heaven up here."

She turned to follow his gaze. "I like the view, just not the road getting here."

"There's another route. It's less steep, but a longer drive."

"Which would be my choice."

"That's the one my uncle needs to use. He still has his license, but he shouldn't be on the front mountain road. It's winding and steep and much too dangerous."

"Promise we'll use the other road when we leave here."

Everett nodded. "If you insist."

Dropping the bags on the porch, he rapped on the door. "I doubt he's still awake."

When no one answered, he bent over a flowerpot, moved the stoneware and held up a key. "Uncle Harry kept his door unlocked for years. I talked him into being a bit more cautious, but he insists on hiding a key outside, just in case."

"My roommate did the same."

"Denise hid a key?"

She nodded. Her eyes widening. "The killer could have known that."

"Could have known or could have hunted around in hopes she was like a lot of other people who worry about being locked out of their homes."

"The boyfriend would have known about the key."

Everett nodded. "More than likely she might have mentioned it to him. I'll let Frank know."

Before Everett stuck the key in the lock, the door opened and a big man with a wide smile, laughing eyes and open arms stood in the doorway.

"You must be Natalie."

She stepped into his embrace after a hesitant glance at Everett.

"Nice to meet you, Mr. Kohl."

He gave a big, hearty laugh that filled the night. "I won't know who you're talking to with that Mr. Kohl comment. Folks call me Uncle Harry. Even those who aren't kin." He hugged her tight, then reached for Everett's hand.

"How you doing, son?"

"Fine, sir."

As Natalie stepped aside, the two men embraced. Although they were the same height, Everett was muscular in areas when his uncle had turned a bit soft. The one man's face was lean and angular where the welcoming uncle's round cheeks, crinkled eyes and wide smile reminded Natalie of a Saint Nick of sorts. For a moment she forgot the reason they had come to the mountains and the need to hide out.

"Come in." Harry stepped back and motioned them into his home.

She was pleasantly surprised by the homey ambience. Wooden antiques and overstuffed furniture in warm hues invited her in.

A stone fireplace was flanked by two comfy chairs with matching ottomans that begged to be used. The round braided rug between the chairs stretched to the couch and oversize coffee table. A leather-bound Bible, a few magazines featuring Georgia settings on the cover, a stack of books and a candy dish filled with individually wrapped chocolates added to the pleasant aura of the room.

The smell of fresh-brewed coffee and something Italian wafted past her and made her mouth water.

"The coffee's hot," Uncle Harry announced, pointing them through the main room and into the adjoining dining area and kitchen beyond.

"Baked spaghetti is warming in the oven, if you're hungry." He glanced at Natalie. "How long since you've last eaten?"

"Breakfast some hours ago."

He raised an eyebrow at Everett. "You forgot how to buy a lady lunch, son?"

"We were in a hurry, sir."

"Don't blame Everett. He wanted to stop, but I insisted we keep driving." She inhaled the bountiful aroma. "Baked spaghetti sounds wonderful. May I help by setting the table?"

Harry nodded. "Silverware's in the drawer closest to the sink. Plates are overhead." He handed two quilted hot mitts to Everett. "Pull that casserole out of the oven, son, and place it on the wooden cutting board. There's bagged lettuce in the fridge and an assortment of dressings."

After arranging the silverware on the table, Natalie filled a large bowl with salad and carried it to the table along with three types of dressing, salt-and-pepper shakers and grated Parmesan cheese.

"There's French bread on the counter," Uncle Harry added.

"Shall I warm it in the microwave?" she asked.

"Sounds good," Harry said with a nod. "I'm not used to having company this far up the mountain."

"Except for Mrs. Beyer who likes to check up on you." Everett turned to Natalie and winked. "Did she make the spaghetti casserole?"

Uncle Harry feigned being hurt. "You don't think I prepared it myself?"

Everett chuckled. "I'm well aware of your many talents, my dear uncle, and cooking anything that smells and looks this good isn't one of them."

Harry slapped his nephew's back playfully. "You know me too well. Bessie heard you were coming for a visit and insisted she provide food to tide us both over." He laughed. "She was thinking of your well-being, Everett. By the way, your dad called me today."

"Everything okay?"

"He wanted to see if I was ready to move to the city." The smile slip from the older man's face. "I told him I hadn't made up my mind about moving."

Everett patted his uncle's shoulder. "You'll know when it's the right time."

"Your father said this is a good time to sell my house, but I'm just not sure if this is the right time for me to move."

"I understand."

"Do you?" Harry pursed his lips. "Hard to know how it feels to have to leave a house you've lived in for so many years. The memory of my wife is here. I can sense her with me. Don't know if she'll cotton to a change of location."

"I doubt she'd forsake you, Uncle Harry."

"Maybe not, but I don't want her to think that I'm forsaking her." He walked to the window and looked into the dark night. "She loved the view up here. Said it made her feel close to God. 'Spect she's with Him now and probably doesn't need the view, but it warms my heart to wake in the morning and see the valley below."

"Winter's coming, Uncle Harry. The roads are bad. You'll go days if not weeks without seeing anyone. If you got sick or needed to go to the hospital—"

The older man nodded and turned abruptly back to the kitchen. "Then I'd be in a difficult position. I understand that, Everett, but I still don't like the idea of moving."

Natalie smiled. "It's hard to leave a place you love."

Harry nodded, his eyes narrowed, and he patted her arm as he passed. "You're a woman of wisdom, Natalie. I've only just met you, but you remind me of my wife." He glanced at Everett. "Might be someone to get to know better, son. You could use a good woman in your life."

Everett sputtered. "Ah, yes, sir."

Natalie's cheeks burned. Uncle Harry's comment had put them both in a very awkward position.

"Everett and I are working on a case," she quickly inserted. "As soon as he gets more evidence, he'll head back to Fort Rickman."

"And you?" the older man asked.

"I'll need to go someplace, but I'm not sure where at this point."

"Then you probably understand the way I feel about not wanting to leave my home."

She nodded. "I understand about not having a home to call your own."

Seeing Everett's unease, she motioned to the table. "Why don't we eat before the casserole gets cold?"

Everett held a chair for her as she grabbed the bread from the microwave and slipped into a seat across from him and next to Harry.

The older man held out his hands. She followed Everett's lead and placed her hands in theirs.

Uncle Harry lowered his head and closed his eyes. "Father, thank You for my family." He squeezed Natalie's hand, making her feel included. "Everett and Natalie are so thoughtful to visit me when I'm struggling with this decision to leave my home. Strengthen all of us for what lies ahead. Nourish our bodies with this food and let us rest tonight so we're able to serve You in the day ahead. Amen."

"Your prayer was perfect," Natalie said, reaching for the fork.

Tomorrow would be a new day. What would it bring? Hopefully, answers and new evidence that would identify the killer. She wanted to go home. When she tried to swallow the first bit of spaghetti, it lodged in her throat. She didn't have a home. Her apartment was a murder scene and she had no place to turn.

What would tomorrow bring? She didn't know. Did God? If so, He wasn't willing to share anything with her. Not now, not when she wasn't sure He was interested in her well-being. At least she had Everett, but was he interested in her or only his investigation?

Everett insisted Uncle Harry go to bed after they had eaten, and then he showed Natalie to a guest room upstairs. "I'll sleep downstairs on the couch. Holler if you need anything."

She placed her bag on the floor near the bed and then followed him back to the kitchen. "I need to help tidy up. You get the bedding you need while I wash the dishes and return the rest of the casserole to the refrigerator."

Everett carried the plates to the sink. "We'll work together if you insist. You must be exhausted."

"And you aren't?"

"I'm used to going for periods of time without sleep. It goes with the job."

"Do you ever go off the clock?"

He shook his head. "You know the military's a 24/7 type of job."

"I know you need to take time for yourself. What's your idea of fun?"

He hesitated. "Jogging relaxes me. I lift weights three times a week."

"I said fun, Everett, not PT."

He laughed. "I like to hike the mountain trails."

"Maybe you'll find time for that tomorrow."

"Join me?"

She shook her head. "If it involves walking along that steep ridge, I'll stay here with Uncle Harry. I told you how I feel about heights."

"We could find an area that's a bit more level and away from the mountain's edge."

Stepping closer, he took the dirty dishes from her hands.

Her heart skittered. "I'm not sure I can trust you."

The look in his gaze made her wish things were different.

"Have I done anything to not earn your trust?" he asked. "Have I hurt you in any way?"

She inhaled quickly. "Of course not."

"Then why can't you trust me?"

She turned back to the dishes. "It's a problem I have from my past."

"I'm not your parents."

She hesitated, then, turning, she wiped her hands dry on a dish towel. "You're not them, but you're an investigator, and the CID thinks I'm guilty of murdering two women. That puts me in a very difficult position."

"Tonight we're far away from Fort Rickman. You said I needed some downtime. Why don't we both try to put the investigation behind us?"

"And forget that you're a CID agent and I'm a possible suspect?"

"A person of interest," he corrected.

"Are you sure you can shove aside the investigation?"

He stepped closer and took her hands, then, placing them on his shoulders, he pulled her closer. The scent of her perfume made him dizzy with interest. He stared down at her, noticing the blueness of her eyes and the smoothness of her skin. Her lips parted ever so slightly, and he lowered his mouth to hers. The sweetness of her kiss made him want to draw her even closer and wrap her more tightly in his embrace.

A voice of reason sounded a warning in the back of his mind, but he shoved the thought aside and soaked in the freshness of her kiss and the warmth of her closeness.

She pulled back. "I don't think this is according to military policy."

He couldn't help but smile. "You're worried it might be taken for fraternization?"

"Something like that."

"But you're no longer in the military. I don't see how it could be a problem."

She pushed away from him and shook her head. "Tell that to your boss at CID Headquarters."

"Chief Agent-in-Charge Craig Wilson is out of town. Frank Gallagher is holding down the fort while the boss is gone."

All the levity drained from Natalie's face. "Frank's the one who thinks I'm involved with the murders."

Everett inhaled sharply. She was right. The investigation was ongoing. What was he thinking to let himself get carried away?

"Frank's a good man, but he's under a lot of pressure. The evidence will prove your innocence."

"And until then, I'm not the person you should be kissing." She sighed. "It's late. The food is put away, and the dishes are done. I'm heading upstairs to get some sleep. I suggest you do the same."

"If there's anything you need..." If she was

fearful or worried or needed someone to hold her, he'd be downstairs standing guard, struggling to come to terms with his actions and his thoughts. He'd never felt this mixed-up, certainly never while investigating a case.

"I'll see you in the morning." She hurried into the living room and then scurried up the stairs, her footfalls nearly silent on the hardwood staircase.

Stepping into the main room, he watched as she slipped into the guest room. The door shut quietly behind her, leaving an emptiness in the night that made him groan.

What was he thinking? He never should have gotten so close to her. The scent of her perfume had done something to his resolve, that and the silky softness of her skin. When he'd looked into her eyes, he'd only seen her beauty and not all the confusion that swirled around her.

Turning back to the sink, he let out the water and wiped his hands before he headed to the hall closet and pulled out two sheets, a blanket and pillow. He wouldn't get much sleep tonight, but not because he was on the couch. Rather because he could look up the A-frame to the loft and see the door to the guest room where she slept. Surely, she was safe here. Safe from the man in the dark sedan and the person who had shot the window in the fishing cabin. Were they one and the same?

The killer wouldn't be able to follow them to the mountain. If he did, he'd have to get past Everett first. He wouldn't let anyone hurt Natalie.

Then he thought of the kiss and the way his heart had reacted to her nearness. Hopefully, Natalie wouldn't get hurt. Hopefully, Everett wouldn't get hurt, either.

SEVENTEEN

Natalie woke to the bright glow of sunlight streaming through the curtains. She sighed, trying to relive the dream she'd had. Everett had kissed her, and the warmth of his lips and the intensity of his kiss had made her melt until she wasn't sure her legs could support her. She'd wanted to stay wrapped in his arms until the light of day had pulled her fully from her slumber.

Sitting up, she wiped her hand over her face and then startled, realizing her dream had been a repeat of what had really happened last night.

She threw her legs over the side of the bed and sighed with regret. The kiss had been better than she had ever imagined. No wonder she wanted to slip back to sleep and reenact the special moment of closeness.

She shook her head. They'd both been too tired and not thinking rationally last night.

Today they'd be back to a very proper relationship of CID agent and suspect.

Person of interest, she corrected herself.

Padding to the guest bathroom, she quickly showered and changed into a fleece top and jeans. The fresh outfit did wonders for her morale, as did her washed hair that she quickly blow-dried. After adding a bit of lipstick and blush, she smiled at her reflection in the mirror before she made the bed and returned all her items to the overnight tote.

She thought of Uncle Harry as she opened the curtains and took in the beauty of the mountain scenery. One window faced the manicured yard behind the house. Another opened to the valley that stretched out below them, aglow with autumn colors. She understood how his wife would have loved living on top of the world. Perhaps they were close to God, after all.

I've never given You much thought, Lord, but Everett has a deep faith, as does his uncle. Maybe I have everything wrong. Forgive me for being so shortsighted, and if You can hear me, let all things come together for good.

Opening the door, she smiled, inhaling the smell of bacon and coffee. The sound of two male voices greeted her as she hurried down the stairs.

"Morning, sleepyhead," Everett teased as she entered the kitchen.

Uncle Harry pulled a mug from the cabinet. "I hope you slept well, Natalie. Care for some coffee?"

She smiled and accepted the mug he offered. "Coffee's just what I need, and I slept like a log." Laughing at the phrase she hadn't used since she was a kid, she pulled a carton of milk from the refrigerator and poured a hefty dollop into her cup.

"Breakfast smells delicious," she said, lifting the cup of hearty brew to her lips.

"That's Everett's doing," Uncle Harry said with pride. "He told me to stand back and let him play short-order cook."

"What would you like, ma'am?" Everett asked with a bow, making her feel special in a fun, lighthearted way. "Eggs, bacon, toast, grits? Or all of the above?"

"Yes, yes, yes and yes. All of the above." She pulled open the silverware drawer. "Since you've done all the cooking, the least I can do is set the table."

Everett divided the food onto three plates and settled across from Natalie at the table.

Uncle Harry again offered a blessing before they all ate hungrily.

"You've done the family proud," Uncle Harry said with a nod of his head as he finished the last of his eggs and swallowed them down with the rest of his coffee.

Returning his cup to the table, he glanced at Natalie. "Everett said you two are taking a hike into the mountains today."

She raised her brow at the playful cook. "Is that what you told your uncle?"

He winked, which sent a zap of warmth to her midsection. "Isn't that what we talked about last night?"

His eyes held a mischievousness that tingled her toes and made her return his innocent gaze with laughter. "We talked about a lot of things. I remember mentioning my fear of heights."

"Take the back canyon trail, Everett. You'll be away from the cliffs. The trail's well marked and easy hiking." He glanced at Natalie. "You've got walking boots?"

"Just tennis shoes, but I don't plan to go far."

"That's not what Everett told me."

Seeing her confusion, Everett laughed and threw up his hands. "It's a plot to get me in trouble. Uncle Harry, you're spreading stories about me."

"You're a fine young man, Rett. No need to apologize for wanting to spend time with Natalie. If I were your age, I'd give you a run for your money."

She laughed. "I'd only have eyes for you, Uncle Harry."

"Hey." Everett acted hurt. "Where's that leave me?"

"In the dust," Harry said, poking his nephew's arm playfully.

Working together, they quickly rinsed the dishes and put them in the dishwasher.

Everett took a few water bottles from the fridge and shoved them into a backpack, along with two protein bars.

"I'll grab a sweater." She raced back upstairs and returned to find Everett in the living room, his cell to his ear.

The tight expression on his face made her pause at the foot of the stairs. She didn't want to eavesdrop, but she also wanted to know who had called. Was it the CID from Germany or Special Agent Frank Gallagher?

"Did you notify anyone at Fort Rickman?" Everett asked, turning to nod in her direction. "You're sure about that?"

He held the cell close to his ear. "Anything turn up on a dark sedan?" He paused, listening. "If I'd gotten the license, we would have tracked him down by now."

Another pause. "That's right. Contact me if anything else develops."

He disconnected and shoved his phone into his pocket. "Vernon Ingalls did not commit suicide."

"The autopsy confirmed his death was a homicide?" she asked.

"That's right. The toxicology screen came back positive. More definitive testing will be done. The results will take longer."

"And the iced tea?"

"Positive, as well. A date-rape drug. Easy to acquire, especially in the city, and effective."

"What about the suicide note?" Natalie asked.

"The key type didn't match any of the printers at Vernon's office. They're searching other sources. If they locate the printer, they'll also locate the killer."

"Frank needs to check Mason Yates's home and the printers at the CID office."

Everett nodded. "That's being done. They're also checking Wanda's printer."

"Did she give them permission?"

"She did."

Natalie swallowed the bile that filled her

throat. "Frank wasn't concerned about Wanda. He was questioning whether I was involved. Did they check the printer in Denise's apartment?"

Everett nodded. "And the printers at the restaurant where Denise worked."

"All of them were ruled out?"

"That's exactly right."

"So who wrote the note?"

Everett shook his head. "No clue at this point. The police officer said he'd notify me if anything else comes to light."

"And Frank. What's he say?"

"He was in a meeting when I called earlier this morning. The special agent I spoke to said they're no closer now to knowing who was involved than at the very beginning."

"And Mason?"

"He's hasn't been taken into custody."

"Has he remained on post?"

"I won't know until I talk to Frank."

"Why haven't they questioned Mason?"

"There's not enough concrete evidence, Natalie."

"Except everything I told you." She tapped her foot and clenched her jaw. "Frank doesn't want to admit that Mason could be a murderer." She stared at Everett. "What do you think? Is Mason guilty?"

"You've provided enough information."

"But you're ignoring what I said."

Everett shook his head. "I'm waiting to hear back from Frank."

She threw up her hands. "How long do we have to wait?"

"I'll call him now."

He punched in the number. Natalie's stomach dropped. Had she pushed Everett too far? Everything had started out good this morning. For a short time, she had escaped the ominousness that had surrounded her since she'd heard the argument at Fort Rickman.

She turned to glance out the window. The weather had changed. Dark clouds hung over the valley and warned of inclement weather and a possible storm. In addition, a storm was brewing within her.

"Frank, this is Everett."

Natalie rubbed her hands, wondering what the conversation would reveal. So much had happened. Too much.

Everett quickly filled Frank in on what Janet Queen had shared last night. Although the CID agent was interested, he had even more important information to share with Everett. Information Everett didn't like hearing.

After disconnecting, he pocketed his cell and walked past Natalie on his way to the porch.

She followed him outside. "What did he say?"

Everett stared at the dark clouds in the distance. They wouldn't be able to take that hike. No telling what would have happened if the storm had hit with them far from his uncle's house.

"What's wrong, Everett?" Natalie asked when he failed to respond. "Is there something you don't want me to know?"

"You told me your relationship with your mother wasn't good, but you failed to mention what happened the night you graduated high school."

Pain slashed across her face. "What do you mean?"

"I mean the night you pushed her down the stairs."

She shook her head. "I did no such thing."

"According to a police officer who Frank happens to know—a guy who worked in Detroit and remembered being called to an inner-city home in the projects."

She shook her head. "Cops rarely came to my area of the city."

He raised his brow and stared at her. "They did when your mother said her daughter had tried to kill her."

Natalie's eyes sparked fire. "How did Frank find this cop? Seems a bit suspect to me since he won't even question Mason."

"He knew the guy's brother, who was in the army."

"Does he always believe everything other people tell him?"

"Of course not. What's the real story?"

"I told you I grew up in a dysfunctional home. My mother pushed my father around. The night of my graduation, my mother slapped me. Usually alcohol made him docile. This time it had an opposite effect. He shoved her away from me. She was standing on a small rug by the door to the basement. She turned abruptly, and her foot caught on the rug. She fell down the stairs."

"Who called the police?"

Natalie pointed a finger back at her chest. "I called for help. Only when they arrived, my mother claimed I had pushed her."

"And your father?"

"He went along with her."

"Did they press charges?"

"My mother wanted to. My father eventually admitted it had been accidental."

"Evidently, the call that night made an impression on the police officer. Frank said he was a rookie, new on the job. The first time anything happens you tend to remember."

He thought of his own first case of sexual harassment, involving the female soldier and the sergeant major. He hadn't looked hard enough or deep enough.

He glanced at Natalie. Was he making another mistake in this case?

Natalie hurried back into the house. Her morale was at low ebb. She'd thought Everett believed in her, but the phone call from Frank made her realize how mistaken she'd been.

She'd left Detroit as a young girl and had enlisted as soon as she turned eighteen. The army had been good for her and provided a way out of the inner city. She'd flourished under the rules and regulations and taken pride in her ability to move up the enlisted ranks.

Looking out the window at the valley below, she raised her hand to her lips, trying to hold back the pain she felt. Everything had been going so well until the woman in Germany had died. Something had changed with Mason. Prior to the death investigation, he'd barely noticed her. Following the woman's fall, Mason had taken a very definite interest in her, one that she had tried to ignore at first. His comments and interest escalated so Natalie did everything in her power to elude him and prevent them from ever being alone together.

She shook her head. What had changed? If he and the woman were having an affair and he killed her, why would he quickly turn his attentions to Natalie as if he had been slighted and was on the rebound? Nothing made sense then, and it still didn't.

"Natalie?" Uncle Harry called to her.

She hurried to see if he was okay and smiled when she saw him trying to pull a scrapbook out of the hall closet.

"I wanted you to see pictures of my wife."

Taking the book from his hands, she placed it on the dining room table.

Everett was still outside, the cell once again glued to his ear. No telling with whom he was talking now.

She shook off her own unease and settled into a straight-back chair next to the delightful man, who began to recount stories about pictures of his sweet Rosie, as he called her.

"Here's Everett with my wife when he was a boy."

Natalie leaned in closer to see a skinny kid with big eyes and a wide smile dressed in a child's army costume.

"Looks like he always liked the military."

Uncle Harry nodded. "Since he was a little guy. He wanted to be a policeman, too, so the CID was a nice fit."

Pictures followed that showed Everett growing into a handsome teen. In one photo, he stood with his arm around a young girl in a sparkly dress. "When was this picture taken?"

"Everett's senior prom. His mother sent photos. She said the girl was nice, but the kids were just friends."

"Did Everett ever fall in love?" Natalie was surprised by the question that slipped out of her mouth without forethought.

Harry nodded. "Once. He was serious, bought a ring. She didn't like the military and ran off with another man."

Natalie felt for Everett. She hadn't gone to prom. No one had asked her, but she didn't have money for a fancy dress so the lack of an invitation was a blessing of sorts.

"I've never been in love," she admitted.

"Really?" His eyes were warm when he

stared down at her. "Maybe you were afraid to let yourself love. There's nothing to fear and everything to gain."

"You're alone now. Don't you get sad since your wife is gone?"

He nodded. "But the memories bring joy even when I feel lonely. I wouldn't trade my years with Rosie for anything."

He stared at a photo of Everett climbing on the rocks behind his house. "Everett said he'd never love again, but I know that's just talk. He's got such a big heart, and a need to protect and defend. I can't see him being alone for the rest of his life."

"I'm sure he'll find a special woman."

"Hopefully, he'll realize how special she is when he finds her."

Everett opened the door and stepped inside, bringing a stiff wind with him. "The storm is approaching. I'm glad we're here instead of climbing the hills."

Uncle Harry's eyes narrowed. "*The Farmer's Almanac* said we're in for a stormy fall and cold winter. I need to check the toolshed out back and the lawn furniture on the deck."

"I'll help you," Everett said. "Just tell me what to do."

The two men disappeared, leaving Natalie alone to stare at the photos in the album.

Her heart was heavy, seeing Uncle Harry with his arm around his wife. Her full cheeks and glittering eyes touched Natalie. That was the type of love she'd want if she ever found anyone she could believe in.

Glancing over her shoulder and through the kitchen window, she saw Everett carrying a wrought-iron chair into the attached garage. Uncle Harry pointed to a small table and folding chair that needed to be taken into the shelter and then raised his gaze and stared at the blackening sky.

Natalie should help them, but she glanced again at the photos and couldn't pull her eyes from a snapshot of a lovely family. Everett stood next to a tall man, who was probably his dad. Pride was evident on the older man's face as he held his wife close and wrapped his other arm over his son's shoulder. A pretty woman— no doubt, Everett's sister—sat in front of the threesome, holding a small infant.

Natalie was overcome with sorrow for what she never had growing up. The way her life was going, it was doubtful she'd ever experience the love and acceptance so clearly evident in the photo.

Everett was a lucky man in so many ways.

If only she could tap into some of the affirmation he'd received growing up. He had his feet on the ground, which was where Natalie wanted hers to remain.

Once the storm passed, she'd make plans to strike out on her own. She didn't need Everett. She didn't need Uncle Harry. The only person she needed was herself.

Then, realizing her mistake, she closed the scrapbook and scooted away from the table.

She needed something in her life and someone. Someone like Everett. But he wasn't interested in a woman on the run who was a person of interest.

He needed and wanted a stable home life, and a wife of whom he could be proud. Natalie was neither.

She was just passing through his life for a small fraction of time. Tomorrow she'd be gone, and Everett could go on with his life. He'd be wiser and better off without her. But what about Natalie?

Would she always have a hole in her heart?

Could Everett have filled that space?

Maybe once upon a time, but not now.
Hopefully, he'd find that special someone.
Hopefully, she'd find that special person, as well.

EIGHTEEN

What had seemed warm and wonderful this morning was quickly turning into something as dark as the clouds rolling over the valley.

Natalie wanted sunshine and blue skies, not storms and wind and a chilly breeze that whipped up from the side of the mountain.

"We need to drive back to Fort Rickman," Everett said, his eyes cold and unreadable.

"What about Mason?"

"Frank plans to question him."

"He needs to be held and interrogated, not asked a few questions that may or may not have relevance on this case."

She shook her head and wrapped her hands around her waist. "You don't realize what you're doing. You're leading me back to Mason. He's manipulative. That's what Janet confirmed. He'll find a way to elude apprehension, and he'll come after me."

"I'll protect you."

"How?" A lump filled her throat, but she refused to give in to the tears that welled close to the surface. She wanted to lean on Everett and accept his help and support. She thought there was something growing between them, something other than the animosity she felt now.

"You can't be with me 24/7. Where will I go? My apartment is a crime scene. I can't stay there. Wanda is still holed up someplace with Sofia. She doesn't need me in her life, especially if Mason remains on the loose. If I had anyone in Detroit, I'd go back there."

Everett sighed with exasperation. "I'll find a safe place for you to stay. We'll have the military police guard you."

"You don't have enough personnel. Plus, where would you have me hide out? At the Lodge on post? That's where Mason was staying unless his house has been made right and he can return to his quarters." She shivered. "How could he go back into that house after killing his wife there and throwing her down the stairs?"

"There are hotels in town."

"Fleabag hotels where Mason could con the night clerk out of the key to my room. I'll need to get a gun and a watchdog. My car's still at the fishing cabin."

"We can stop there on the way to post."

She turned away from Everett, unwilling to accept the change in him. Why wouldn't he listen to her? He had seemed like the perfect gentleman. He opened doors for her and scooted in her chair at the table. He prayed before they ate and said he believed in God, but he didn't believe in her. He was still a CID agent who listened to his supervisor even when the information he'd been given was wrong.

Natalie raced from the room. Everett tried to grab her arm, but she jerked out of his hold. She climbed the stairs to the bedroom and slammed the door behind her. Standing with her back to the wall, she let the tears fall. She cried for the dreams of her youth that never came true. Maybe her mother was right—she wasn't good enough or smart enough to make something of her life.

Her mother said the inner city would follow her, that she had a stench about her from growing up poor, a stench that wouldn't wash off no matter how hard she tried to come clean.

Her father hadn't negated what her mother had said, so he must have believed it, too. The bottle was his answer, but Natalie didn't want to escape life, she wanted to live it.

She'd had a glimpse of how good things could be. She'd seen the love in Uncle Harry's eyes, and the way he smiled when he talked about his wife. That's what she wanted. Someone to love her and honor her and say that she was his special treasure.

But she wasn't special. She was soiled from the inner city. Her past would always follow her. She couldn't escape.

Everett wanted to haul her back to post. He might even trick her into thinking that she was no longer a person of interest and then arrest her once they were on the military post.

She couldn't trust him.

She couldn't trust anyone.

"Oh, God," she cried out. "Can I even trust You?"

Everett's heart twisted in two as he watched Natalie run up the stairs and slam the door to the bedroom.

Uncle Harry stuck his nose in from the kitchen. "Everything okay?"

Everett sighed. "Nothing is right at this point."

"You got heartache, son."

"How's that?"

"Your heart's aching 'cause you like that lovely young woman. Appears to me that she feels the same about you."

Everett shook his head. "This isn't about hearts, it's about heads and a murder investigation and bringing the guilty to justice."

"Maybe your head is focused on that, but your heart is interested in another facet of this situation. Natalie's a wonderful girl. I've seen the way she looks at you and the way you smile back at her. Take this morning when you were fixing breakfast. I stuck around just to watch cupid hit you over the head. Seems you're both affected."

"Cupid? What are you talking about?"

"When I met your Aunt Rose, I couldn't think straight for three weeks. Kept walking around in circles until my dear dad told me to ask her out. I was afraid she'd want nothing to do with me. Turns out those three weeks she'd been crying at night wondering why I wasn't interested."

"Natalie might be crying, but it's from anger. She refuses to return to Fort Rickman. She's doesn't trust me."

"Have you earned her trust?"

"What's that mean?"

"Did you tell her you'd take care of everything, and then do a one-eighty and change your mind? She's scared and all alone. She needs you now more than you can ever imagine."

"I'm being told to bring her back."

"What's your heart say?"

"My heart says I don't know what to think. Everywhere I turn she seems to be involved in this case, yet I know she's not. Maybe my problem is that I can't believe my own instincts."

"Give it time. Call post. Tell them to wait until this evening. Follow some of your own leads while I do what I can."

"What's that?"

He grabbed a Bible off his bookshelf. "I'm spending time with the Lord. He has a way of sorting through the problems and giving right judgment to those who ask His help. Have you turned to Him?"

Everett felt crestfallen. He hadn't prayed in so long, other than to utter a blessing over food or to ask a quick prayer for help, always on his terms and for his own need. Maybe this was the time and place to seek the Lord's counsel.

He reached for the Bible. "Mind if I use this for a while? I'll be out back in that swing you made for Aunt Rose."

Harry smiled as he glanced out the window. "Looks like we've got some time before the storm rolls this way. The temperature might be a little cool, but that should clear your head. Take all the time you need."

Everett left the house and settled into the double swing. The creak of the wood and the gentle sway washed away his initial upset. He opened the Bible and then closed his eyes before he read any of the text, just letting his hand lie on the page. *Forgive me, Lord, and lead me.*

The breeze blew his hair and a hawk circled overhead, as Everett poured out his heart.

Don't let me make another mistake, dear God. Direct my steps according to Your holy will. Help me see clearly and know what's best for Natalie and best for this investigation. Help me to do the right thing, above all else.

NINETEEN

Natalie heard a tap at her door and for a moment hoped it was Everett. Instead, she found Uncle Harry with a steaming mug in hand.

"I thought a cup of tea might help and a little conversation."

She smiled, accepted the mug. "You're so thoughtful. Come in."

He slipped past her and glanced out the window that faced the backyard. "Everett's got a lot on his mind."

She peered around Uncle Harry's shoulder. "He's reading?"

"The Word."

"Maybe God will help him realize he needs to think for himself."

"That's something he's struggling with."

"The case is a tough one."

"I don't think the case is the main problem." He turned and smiled down at her. "He's a good man. Something happened when he first started with the CID. I don't know all the details. He took two weeks leave and came here to spend time away."

Uncle Harry pointed to the window. "He spent a lot of time doing just what he's doing now. Praying, meditating, asking the Lord what he should do. He thought about getting out of the military and ending his career in law enforcement. A woman had died. Her death played heavily on his heart. He felt responsible when he had been ordered to end the case. He knew more could have been uncovered if he'd been given more time."

"The military demands that its people follow orders."

"That's what I told him. He said he needed to follow a higher call, as well, that he'd questioned the order but hadn't stood his ground."

"He was young."

"Exactly."

"This is different, Uncle Harry."

"Of course it is, child." He patted her shoulder and headed to the door. "But you need to know that he's struggling."

He stepped from the room and closed the door behind him. Natalie turned back to the window and stared down at Everett.

He'd made a mistake. She'd made many growing up, trying to prove her self-worth to parents who didn't have faith in her. *A child who doesn't receive love doesn't know how to give love.* She sighed, realizing she still struggled with opening herself enough to love another. She'd had to make her way in life, to succeed, to take care of herself.

Now she was being asked to subjugate her own needs for the needs of another. Everett had a need to take her back to Fort Rickman, which could be her undoing.

She was at a crossroads. Would she run away and try to start a new life for herself? Or should she go with Everett and believe he knew what was best?

A hard decision. One she didn't know how to make.

The old poem about two roads diverging and not knowing which path to take came to mind. If only she could see beyond the here and now.

God, You know all. Direct my steps. I'm seeing with finite eyes, but Yours are infinite. Help me to choose the right path.

Do I choose Everett or do I walk away from him and make my own way in the world, all alone?

* * *

Everett closed the Bible and rose from the swing, still as confused as ever. Wasn't prayer supposed to bring peace? This time it left him even more unsettled.

Pulling his cell from his pocket, he tapped in the number for the CID agent in Germany.

"I'm at a crossroads here in Georgia, Tyler. I thought you might provide new insight."

"Your timing's perfect. We've received the report from the German police, which included an eye-witness account. One of my guys is fluent in German and did the translation."

"What'd you find?"

"The witness saw a woman at Paula Conway's apartment early in the morning before the police arrived on the scene. She had black hair and was in a military uniform."

"Military? US or German?"

"She was one of ours. She came out of the front door and climbed into a small red car."

Everett thought of Natalie's car.

"The witness had seen her before, driving back and forth to work each day." Tyler hesitated. "Anything ring a bell?"

"What do you mean?"

"You mentioned Natalie Frazier when you

first called me. Natalie lived down the street from Paula Conway. She drove a red sedan."

"Are you saying she was the woman seen that morning?"

"I'm saying she appears to have been there before the German police arrived at the house."

"Tammy Yates was supposedly called to check on Paula, so I don't understand why Natalie would have been there."

Tyler sniffed. "Was Natalie checking on the teacher or had she killed the woman and wanted to make sure she hadn't left anything behind?"

Everett couldn't—and wouldn't—believe Natalie was involved. "Did you get the witness's name? I want you to verify the report. Something's wrong."

"Here's the problem. The witness was visiting someone in the area, and we don't have contact information."

"So you can't track him down?"

"Not a him," Tyler said. "It's a female. The *polizei*'s penmanship is hard to read, but the name appears to be Anna Bell."

"What?" Everett tried to put the pieces together. "Tyler, that's not two names, it's one. Annabelle Yates."

"Any relation to Mason?"

"It's his sister. And she's lying."

TWENTY

Heavyhearted, Natalie stepped onto the porch, where Uncle Harry stood looking over the valley.

"I don't want to leave my home," he said, his voice husky with emotion.

"Have you reserved a room at the assisted-living facility in Atlanta?"

He nodded. "Only because my brother—Everett's father—convinced me it was time to move. He's worried about me. Says the mountain is too lonely."

She touched his arm. "Are you lonely?"

He shook his head. "I feel Rosie's presence here." He extended his hand. "When I look over the valley, it's almost as if I'm seeing it through her eyes, as if she's part of me here."

"Have you thought of other options?"

He turned, his brow knit together. "Like what?"

"Getting a caregiver who could help with some of the chores, perhaps fix meals for you when you don't feel like cooking. Someone to go to the store for you when the weather's bad."

"You mean a babysitter?" he spat out.

"Of course not. A companion to help you."

He shook his head. "I doubt anyone would be interested in living up here on the mountain. It would take a special type of person."

"But it's beautiful and so peaceful. It's the type of place I've always dreamed of finding."

His shoulders squared for a moment and a twinkle formed in his eyes. "They need teachers at the local county school. You could stay here, and I'd cover your expenses. There's an extra room over the garage you could use."

The thought of living in the beautiful natural setting was inviting, especially if Natalie could travel on the less hazardous road that didn't edge the cliff.

"I've got an exam to take and then student teaching."

"You could student teach up here. It's a consideration."

She smiled. "And one I like."

A car turned into the driveway.

"Were you expecting someone, Uncle Harry?"

He shook his head and squinted. "I don't recognize the driver."

Natalie couldn't either with the glare that reflected off the windshield. Her heart lurched as she thought it might be someone out to do them harm. When the car came to a stop, Annabelle Yates stepped out, and Natalie breathed a sigh of relief. But the woman's expression was anything but friendly.

"Mason's in the area," Annabelle said. "He told me he was coming to get you."

"How did you know where to find me?"

"Everett left this address at work when he signed out on leave. Mason saw it and called me. I wanted to warn you."

"What's Mason planning to do?"

Annabelle shrugged. "He didn't tell me, but I've never heard him so upset."

"Did he confess to killing Tammy?"

"He didn't have to. I put everything together and realized who was at fault."

She glanced nervously over her shoulder. "Come with me, Natalie. We'll take the back road down the mountain to get away from him."

"I'm not leaving Uncle Harry. Besides, Everett's here. I'll be safe with him."

"Mason said Everett's taking you back to Fort Rickman. He could have waited until you were on the road, but he decided you were more vulnerable here."

Everett opened the screen door and stepped onto the porch. "What's all this about?"

"Mason's headed this way," Natalie explained. "Annabelle wants me to leave with her before he arrives."

Everett shook his head. "Why would he come here?"

"He found your uncle's address with your leave information," Annabelle said. "He called to tell me. I hurried to get to you first."

"You could have phoned."

"I did. The call kept failing. Coverage must be a problem up here."

Natalie glanced at Everett and then back to Annabelle. "I appreciate your concern, but I'm not leaving."

"Tell me what you know about your brother," Everett said.

"I know he was interested in Natalie in Germany. I'm not sure if he transferred to Fort Rickman because she lived in the area or not. He never told me, and I never asked."

"What about Paula Conway? You were visiting your brother. What happened?"

Natalie was confused. "You were in Germany?"

"For a short time. I wanted to make sure Mason was okay." Annabelle motioned impatiently to Natalie. "Hurry. You need to come with me now.

Everett held up his hand. "She stays here."

The woman's face twisted. "I want to show you something that might convince you to change your mind."

She leaned into her car. Then, taking a step back, she raised her arm, a gun in hand.

Natalie gasped. "What are you doing?"

Everett pushed his uncle toward the house and shoved Natalie behind a rocking chair that offered some protection but not enough. He drew his weapon, but not in time.

Annabelle fired twice.

Everett gasped. Blood gushed from his side. Behind him, Uncle Harry collapsed to the deck. The old man clutched his chest. Everett pushed on Harry's wound to stem the flow of blood.

Annabelle grabbed Natalie. She screamed and fought to free herself.

The older woman shoved Natalie down the steps, holding the gun to her head.

Everett staggered to his feet. "Let her go."

Annabelle fired again. The bullet hit him in the leg. He lunged forward. Another bullet hit his arm. The SIG Sauer dropped from his hand, but he continued on.

"No." Natalie fought for control of Annabelle's gun. Again the crazed woman aimed at Everett and fired. He collapsed on the drive, his hand outstretched to Natalie.

She screamed his name and clawed at Annabelle, but the woman was too strong. Raising the heavy weapon, she crashed it against Natalie's neck. Her vision blurred. She went limp, falling to her knees.

Annabelle forced her upright and shoved her toward the black sedan. She hefted Natalie into the front seat, grabbed rope from the glove compartment and quickly tied her hands.

The world swirled around her. Natalie floated in and out of consciousness, only partially aware of Annabelle dragging Everett across the gravel driveway.

Huffing from the exertion, she wrapped her arms around his chest and lifted his upper body into the rear seat, then swung his legs in. He moaned in pain.

Natalie glanced back. Tears flowed from her eyes. Everett was bleeding and pale as death.

"No," she cried.

"Shut up." Annabelle slapped her open palm across the back of Natalie's head. Her world went dark. All she heard was a scream that had to have come from her own mouth.

The car door slammed. Annabelle was in the driver's seat.

The engine started.

"Where...are...you taking—"

"You need to get away. Having Everett with you will be good. You tried to go up the mountain trail, but the car went too fast."

"What do you mean?"

"The cliff at the top. It's called Lover's Leap by the locals. Couples have driven over the edge when they couldn't be together in life, like you and Mason. You rejected him when you left Germany."

"What are you talking about?"

"Do you know how hurt he was?"

"He's behind this," Natalie said, trying to understand. "You're trying to protect him. He killed the woman in Germany, just like he killed his wife."

Annabelle laughed as she turned onto the narrow mountain road and accelerated.

Natalie glanced out the window, seeing the steep drop-off. Her stomach roiled.

"I was visiting Mason in Germany when the woman ended their relationship. Tammy didn't know, but my brother confided in me, like he always had. The doctors told me he had abandonment issues because our mother left him. I couldn't let another woman hurt him."

"You killed Paula Conway in Germany?"

"The stairway was steep. One shove and she was gone."

"Did you kill Tammy because she was interested in Vernon Ingalls?"

"She wasn't interested in Vernon romantically. He was a lawyer. She wanted him to handle her divorce."

"Does Mason know you're a murderer?"

Annabelle shook her head. "He only knows that I'm on his side. I love him as if he were my own son. After Mother left, he needed me."

"You killed Vernon and made it look like suicide."

"I told him Tammy planned to visit him and brought a pitcher of the kind of iced tea she liked. I had him taste it. He didn't know it was doctored."

"With drugs?"

Annabelle held the gun in her right hand and

clutched the wheel with the other. "It didn't take long to work. The problem was dragging him into his office and hoisting him into the air. Then I vacuumed his rug and took the iced tea container with me when I left." She smiled with pride. "I thought of everything, including the suicide note."

Natalie worked to free her hands, while keeping her gaze from the steep drop-off and the speedometer.

"Slow down or we'll never make it to the top."

Annabelle chuckled. "I spent vacations in the mountains. You and Everett won't crash until I'm ready."

"You'll die, too."

She shook her head. "I'll jump to safety before you go over the edge."

Natalie noticed the darkening sky. The storm that had bypassed them earlier looked like it was ready to strike. "You'll be caught in the storm without a car."

"I'll call Mason."

"Fort Rickman is more than a four-hour drive from here."

"He's already on his way. I told him what I planned to do. He didn't want me to get in trouble."

"You're psychotic."

"I'm a protective sister. Mason will thank me."

"He'll arrest you and throw you in jail."

"Shut up."

"I won't. You've got to stop."

Feeling the rope ease free, Natalie had a moment of elation, then she glanced over her shoulder and saw Everett, lying motionless. Her heart lurched. Was he still alive?

Everett heard Natalie's voice but couldn't determine where he was. A car, moving too fast, wheels skidding.

He glanced at the side window, seeing the mountain race by. His gut tightened as his memory returned.

Annabelle's voice. "I wanted to kill you instead of your roommate, but she had a gun."

"You shot Denise?"

"I thought it was you."

"Did Mason realize I was in Freemont?"

"Tammy saw you. She called me, upset, knowing you had stalked Mason in Germany."

"I never did."

"I drove to Fort Rickman to stop you, only you weren't at your apartment, so I had to kill your roommate, instead. I bloodied clothes that

I pulled from your closet and threw them in the Dumpster. Video cameras were in the rear of the apartment complex, but I was careful not to show my face. I wore a stocking cap and one of your coats. I wanted them to come after you, and they would have if not for your boyfriend in the backseat."

Annabelle glanced over her shoulder at Everett.

He closed his eyes.

Natalie screamed. "Watch the road."

The car swerved.

Everett tried to think clearly, in spite of the hits to his chest and leg and his too-rapid loss of blood. His left hand throbbed where the bullet had grazed him, but his right hand was unscathed. He reached for the Smith & Wesson strapped to his ankle. The effort was too much for him. He gasped for air.

Natalie turned ever so slightly.

He signaled her with his good hand but kept it out of Annabelle's line of sight.

Natalie nodded her head.

"Annabelle, you need to slow down on that upcoming curve," she warned.

"I don't have to do anything."

Everett got the message. Mustering his strength, he raised up ever so slightly. Seeing the bend in the road, he lunged and grabbed Annabelle's throat before she could react.

Natalie fought her for control of the gun. The left side of the car slammed against the boulders on the side of the mountain. The screech of metal crushing against granite was deafening.

The car swerved, throwing Everett back against the seat. The gun went off. Annabelle groaned and collapsed over the steering wheel.

Natalie grabbed the wheel, lifted her foot over the console and jammed down on the brake pedal. The car skidded across the road. She frantically pumped the brake. The car came to a stop. The engine died.

Raising up, Everett looked out the window. The valley hung hundreds of feet below. The right front of the car teetered over the edge.

"Everett?" Natalie's voice, not more than a whisper.

"Get out, Natalie."

"I… I can't look out the window."

"Push open the driver's door. Crawl over Annabelle."

"I…I can't. You get out first."

He stretched his hand and grabbed the door handle, but it failed to open. "The backdoor caved in when it hit the boulders. It's stuck. You've got to climb out the front."

She shifted her weight.

The car titled even more.

Natalie gasped.

"You can do it," he cautioned.

Slowly and carefully, she reached across the collapsed woman and pushed on the driver's door. It opened. Shoving Annabelle out of the car, Natalie climbed free herself and turned to look at Everett.

"We don't have much time. Take my hand. I'll help you." Then she looked at the angle of the car, and her heart froze. How could Everett get out alive?

The car was poised on the side of the mountain. Natalie couldn't upset the balance. "Everett, climb free."

"I... I can't." He tried to move his injured leg, but it was deadweight.

"Then crawl to the front seat."

"The motion will send the car over the edge. Call for help."

She looked at her phone. "No signal."

Shoving the cell into her pocket, she reached for the handle on the rear door and pulled. "It won't open."

"Pray, Natalie. We need God."

"Lord," she cried out. "Give me the strength of..." She looked through the door. "Who was strong in Biblical days?"

"Samson."

"Lord, make me strong like Samson."

Again she tried the door. "Please, God."

The car shifted again. She was dizzy just thinking of the huge drop-off and how high they were, almost in the clouds.

The wind increased, buffeting the car and making it shudder. The metal chassis groaned as the car rocked in the wind.

She glanced again at Everett. Blood soaked his clothing.

Despair overtook her. Tears stung her eyes.

She thought of the scripture passage the street preacher had used. *I can do all things through Christ who strengthens me.*

She wouldn't give up. Her life had been a series of setbacks, but she'd overcome them. She hadn't let her childhood and her alcoholic father or her manipulative mother pull her into a way of life that was filled with darkness. She'd freed herself from their hold, thanks to the military. When that turned sour because of Mason, she'd chosen another course and pursued her education degree. Again, when she'd been close to achieving her dream, the evil surrounding Mason had returned, but she'd fought back.

God had sent her Everett. She knew that now. He'd tried to save her from Annabelle. He'd invited her into his family so she could feel the love and support from dear Uncle Harry. *O Lord, send him medical help. Don't let him succumb to the gunshot.*

Everett had sacrificed everything for her.

Please, Lord, don't let the darkness win. You are Lord of the light.

The wind ripped past her. The car swayed. Even darker clouds seemed to be barreling down upon them. Any more wind would send Everett crashing over the edge to his death.

She leaned through the front door. "Everett, can you hear me?"

His eyes blinked open.

A rush of relief made even more tears flow. "We've got to work together. Can you use your leg, the one that's not injured? Push on the door from the inside, and I'll tug from out here."

He nodded and raised his leg.

She grabbed the handle on the outside of the door. "I'll count to three."

The wind whipped up from the canyon

below, but instead of rocking the car, it seemed to provide more stability.

A ray of sunlight broke through the clouds. When she glanced at the sky, she had a surge of hope. The storm seemed to be moving past them.

"One. Two. Three."

Everett shoved his leg against the door. Using all her strength, Natalie pulled on the handle, her hands stinging from the effort.

Time stood still for a long moment as they both worked together and then—

The door flew open.

Natalie fell back. The car wobbled.

Scurrying to her feet, she grabbed Everett's good leg and, while carefully lifting the injured one, she pulled him across the seat. He seemed to gather strength and helped scoot himself. Then with one last burst of energy, he was free from the car.

A rush of wind came round the mountain. The car groaned, teetered again and then slowly fell over the edge. The wind howled, and a huge crash sounded as the car hit the rocks below and burst into flame. Black smoke sailed upward with the wind.

Everett collapsed on the ground. Natalie knelt next to him and wrapped him in her arms.

The sound of a car engine made her turn, relieved help had found them. A navy blue sedan rounded the bend and braked to a stop.

Mason stepped from the car.

Her heart stopped.

"Natalie, are you all right?" he asked as if concerned for her well-being.

"Get away from me."

"I didn't do anything wrong. Annabelle killed that woman in Germany, and she pushed Tammy to her death." He stepped closer. "I'm glad she didn't kill you."

Natalie scrambled away from Everett, wanting to divert Mason's attention. "Don't touch me."

"You know I won't hurt you." He reached for her hand.

She scooted back, then glanced over her shoulder at the huge drop-off. Annabelle's gun lay on a rock next to the overhang. Natalie stretched to reach it.

Everett moaned.

Annabelle stumbled to her feet, blood covering her blouse. "I... I told you I'd take care of her, Mason."

His face clouded. "Why'd you do it, Annabelle?"

"Because she refused your love."

"She won't refuse me after we get rid of him." He pointed to Everett, lying motionless on the ground. "We'll say he shot you and hurt Natalie."

"Shoot both of them, Mason. Then I can take care of you."

He snickered. "Why do you think I'd want that, Annabelle?"

"Because I'm all you have." She staggered toward him, clutching her side. With a low groan, she collapsed at his feet.

Mason pulled a gun from his waistband and turned it on Natalie.

"No," she screamed.

"You caused this to happen."

"It wasn't me. It was your sister."

Out of the corner of her eye, she saw Everett claw at his leg.

She needed to keep talking. "Your mother loved you, Mason. She didn't want to leave."

"What?" Confusion washed across his face. "No."

"She fell down the steps to her death. Did you push her?"

"I… I just wanted her to know how much she'd hurt me."

"It was an accident, right?"

Mason nodded. "Annabelle took care of me."

"She's a good sister."

He looked down at her, then aimed his weapon at Natalie.

She gasped. "You won't get away with this, Mason."

Everett pulled a gun from his ankle holster and fired.

Mason's eyes widened. He grabbed his chest and fell next to his sister.

Annabelle reached out her hand and touched his cheek. "My...ba-baby," she whispered.

Natalie grabbed Mason's gun, then ran to Everett and wrapped him in her arms. Hot tears burned her eyes. He was safe, but he'd lost so much blood and needed medical help.

Sirens screamed in the distance. Someone must have seen the car fire and called for help. Would they arrive in time?

She held him close. "Stay with me, Everett. Don't leave me. I know we're meant to be together. God sent you to take care of me when I couldn't go on. Don't slip away. I need you, Everett. I love you and I always will."

TWENTY-ONE

Bessie Beyer gripped Natalie's hand. "The doctor said Harry's going to pull through."

"Oh, Bessie, that's such good news."

"Actually, the doctor said he was too stubborn to die, which made me smile. Evidently he knows Harry better than I thought."

"He's a good man."

"I hope this doesn't mean he'll move to Atlanta. I don't want to lose him."

Natalie squeezed the older woman's hand. "Tell him how you feel. He needs to know."

"He hasn't gotten over his wife yet."

"Her memory was all he had. Now, with you reaching out to him, he'll find a new reason to live."

"I hope you're right."

Bessie hurried back to Harry's bedside while Natalie returned to Everett's room. He'd been taken off the ventilator, but he remained unresponsive.

She slipped into the chair beside his bed and took up the wait as she'd done all night. *Please, Lord. I've only just found him. I need more time with him. More time with both of you.*

Everett groaned.

She grabbed his right hand and squeezed. "Can you hear me?"

His eyes blinked open. His lips twitched into what she wanted to call a smile.

"You're in the hospital. The doctor's performed surgery on your side and leg."

"W-walk?"

"You'll have to recuperate for a period of time, but you'll be fine."

She was sure of it now that he had come out of the darkness. Sunlight poured through the window and bathed them both in light. She stroked his right hand and then leaned close to kiss his cheek.

"You're going to make it, Everett. I won't let anything happen to you. You saved me from Mason and his sister. Both of them were manipulative. Annabelle needed to protect her brother, but he abused women and knew she had killed Paula Conway in Germany."

"You—"

Natalie nodded. "That's right. She almost killed me in front of Vernon Ingalls's house. The stocking cap she wore made me think it was Mason driving the car. When Frank called to check on you, he said they'll both stand trial and may spend the rest of their lives in jail. Plus, they located Denise's boyfriend. A married guy who ran the restaurant where she worked."

"Uncle—"

"Uncle Harry's doing well. Bessie is with him. He seems to be enjoying the attention."

Everett nodded and squeezed her hand.

"Are you trying to let me know that you're enjoying my attention, too?"

Again, his lips quivered into a smile.

"I'm not planning to go anywhere if that's what you're worried about."

She kissed his cheek again.

He sighed with contentment, closed his eyes and drifted back to sleep.

EPILOGUE

Bessie's car pulled into the driveway of Uncle Harry's home. Natalie waved as she stepped from the house to greet her.

"How are the patients?" the older woman asked, climbing from her vehicle.

"Harry's hard to keep down. He's anxious to see you. Everett's doing well. The doctor's been amazed by his progress and said he'll get the staples out of his leg a few weeks ahead of schedule."

"It's all the care you're giving both of them."

Bessie grabbed a large basket from the backseat. As she moved closer, Natalie spied the food, including roast beef and mashed potatoes.

"Dinner looks delicious."

"I knew you needed to get back to post for

your last class. I thought preparing a meal was the least I could do."

"Do I see fresh-baked yeast rolls and apple pie?"

Bessie nodded. "They're Harry's favorites."

"He's going to want you to stay permanently with all those goodies."

Bessie winked. "That's what I'm hoping."

Natalie laughed. "I wouldn't be surprised if that's on his mind, too. He's been smiling non-stop and praising the Lord almost constantly."

"I'm glad."

Natalie nodded. "So am I. You're sure you don't mind checking in on them tomorrow morning? I should be back late afternoon after I finish my final exam."

"Harry said you've almost completed your degree."

"I'll have student teaching, but I've arranged to do that in the local school here."

"When will Everett go back to work?"

"The doctor said in a month to six weeks."

They moved inside. Everett sat on a chair by the fire and reached for a crutch to try to rise.

"Stay where you are," Bessie insisted. "I'm heading to the kitchen to find Harry."

Natalie reached for Everett's hand as she

sat on the hearth next to him and smiled. "I think we'll be seeing a lot of Bessie in the days ahead. Did you have that talk with your uncle about remaining in his home?"

"I didn't need to convince him. He'd already thought about Bessie being close in case he needed help. He's got a new zip to his step and even asked if I thought he was too old to get remarried."

"What'd you tell him?"

"That no one is ever too old for love."

"A perfect answer."

Everett nodded. "I never had time to look for love, Natalie. I was always looking back at the mistake I thought I had made. Since I was shot, I've realized I was following orders, which was what I was supposed to do. I had to forgive myself and forgive my commander at the time. We both could have done more and should have done more, but I can't keep focusing on the past. I'm ready to live in the present."

Her fingers wrapped through his. "I always kept looking over my shoulder, too, Everett, knowing where I'd come from. It didn't matter. What mattered was the type of person I had grown to be. The past had a hold on me only because I wouldn't let it go. Like you, I had to forgive my parents and forgive that young girl who was belligerent and probably hard for her parents to manage at times."

"I call that independence. That's what made you get away and not stay in the middle of their dysfunction."

"Independence sounds better than being an unruly child. Because I was looking back, perhaps some of that darkness kept me from pulling free completely. I know now that I should have registered a sexual harassment complaint against Mason. Perhaps the truth would have come out at that time. Maybe Tammy and Vernon Ingalls would still be alive if I'd done something to stop Mason earlier."

"But you're not to blame for his actions or for what Annabelle did."

She nodded. "I know. I've worked through all of that, and I've put the past behind me." She smiled. "I'm living in the moment, too, and each moment with you is so very special."

Everett's smile warmed her heart.

"I know you've got your exam and student teaching," he said. "I'd never steer you off course. Your career is important. You'll be a wonderful teacher and help so many young children, but—"

She held her breath.

"I'd like to have a place in that future. I haven't gotten out, as you know, to shop so I can't show you a ring—"

She gasped.

"At least not now. Later, we can shop for that together. That is, if you'll say yes."

She tried not to smile and lowered her eyes as if somewhat confused. "But you've never asked me what I should say yes to, the question that needs an answer."

He laughed at his own mistake. "Natalie Frazier, I love you and want to spend the rest of my life by your side. Through sickness—" he pointed down at his leg "—and health."

Her heart melted.

"Would you..." He paused, before asking, "Natalie, would you marry me?"

Tears burned her eyes, but they were tears of joy.

"Oh, Everett." She wrapped her arms around his neck and scooted close as he lowered his lips to hers.

His kiss held the promise of what the future would hold. A life together, with God in the midst of their marriage, through the good times and, yes, even those that wouldn't be as good, but she'd have Everett by her side. She'd left the darkness, and they would both live in the light of God's love, embracing each day to the full.

They'd faced the past and emerged triumphant.

"I'm blessed," she whispered, "to have your love. Yes, Everett. I want to be your wife now and forever."

Uncle Harry's laughter floated from the kitchen as Bessie cooed over him, and the smell of the dinner she'd brought wafted through the living room and filled the house with a tantalizing aroma.

Natalie snuggled closer to Everett. He wrapped her more tightly in his warm embrace and kissed her again, only this time it was long and lingering.

She sighed with pleasure, thinking of their future together, a wonderful future filled with Everett's kisses and his love.

* * * * *

Dear Reader,

I hope you enjoyed *PERSON OF INTEREST*, the eighth book in my Military Investigations Series, which features heroes and heroines in the army's Criminal Investigation Division. Each story stands alone so you can read them in any order, either in print or as an ebook: *THE OFFICER'S SECRET*, book 1; *THE CAPTAIN'S MISSION*, book 2; *THE COLONEL'S DAUGHTER*, book 3; *THE GENERAL'S SECRETARY*, book 4; *THE SOLDIER'S SISTER*, book 5; *THE AGENT'S SECRET PAST*, book 6; and *STRANDED*, book 7.

When a man from her past kills again, college student, Natalie Frazier, fears she may be the next to die. US Army Special Agent Everett Kohl wants to protect her, yet the mistake he made as a rookie investigator still haunts him. Natalie's attempt to make a better life for herself is in question, but by turning to God, she's able to trust Everett with her life…and her heart.

I want to hear from you. Email me at *debby@debbygiusti.com* or write me c/o Love Inspired, 233 Broadway, Suite 1001, New York, NY 10279. Visit my website at *www.Debby-*

Giusti.com, blog with me at *www.seekerville.blogspot.com* and friend me at *www.facebook.com/debby.giusti.9.* As always, I thank God for bringing us together through this story.

Wishing you abundant blessings,
Debby

REQUEST YOUR FREE BOOKS!
2 FREE WHOLESOME ROMANCE NOVELS
IN LARGER PRINT
PLUS 2
FREE
MYSTERY GIFTS

☀ ☀ ☀ ☀ ☀ ☀ ☀ ☀ ☀ ☀ ☀ ☀ ☀ ☀ ☀ ☀ ☀ ☀ ☀

HEARTWARMING™

❀ ❀ ❀ ❀ ❀ ❀ ❀ ❀ ❀ ❀ ❀ ❀ ❀ ❀ ❀ ❀ ❀ ❀ ❀

Wholesome, tender romances

YES! Please send me 2 FREE Harlequin® Heartwarming Larger-Print novels and my 2 FREE mystery gifts (gifts worth about $10). After receiving them, if I don't wish to receive any more books, I can return the shipping statement marked "cancel." If I don't cancel, I will receive 4 brand-new larger-print novels every month and be billed just $5.24 per book in the U.S. or $5.99 per book in Canada. That's a savings of at least 19% off the cover price. It's quite a bargain! Shipping and handling is just 50¢ per book in the U.S. and 75¢ per book in Canada.* I understand that accepting the 2 free books and gifts places me under no obligation to buy anything. I can always return a shipment and cancel at any time. Even if I never buy another book, the two free books and gifts are mine to keep forever.

161/361 IDN GHX2

Name _____ (PLEASE PRINT) _____

Address _____ Apt. # _____

City _____ State/Prov. _____ Zip/Postal Code _____

Signature (if under 18, a parent or guardian must sign)

Mail to the **Reader Service**:
IN U.S.A.: P.O. Box 1867, Buffalo, NY 14240-1867
IN CANADA: P.O. Box 609, Fort Erie, Ontario L2A 5X3

* Terms and prices subject to change without notice. Prices do not include applicable taxes. Sales tax applicable in N.Y. Canadian residents will be charged applicable taxes. Offer not valid in Quebec. This offer is limited to one order per household. Not valid for current subscribers to Harlequin Heartwarming larger-print books. All orders subject to credit approval. Credit or debit balances in a customer's account(s) may be offset by any other outstanding balance owed by or to the customer. Please allow 4 to 6 weeks for delivery. Offer available while quantities last.

Your Privacy—The Reader Service is committed to protecting your privacy. Our Privacy Policy is available online at www.ReaderService.com or upon request from the Reader Service.

We make a portion of our mailing list available to reputable third parties that offer products we believe may interest you. If you prefer that we not exchange your name with third parties, or if you wish to clarify or modify your communication preferences, please visit us at www.ReaderService.com/consumerchoice or write to us at Reader Service Preference Service, P.O. Box 9062, Buffalo, NY 14240-9062. Include your complete name and address.

HW15